Hidden Memories

H I D D E N
MAGIC

B O O K 2

V. R. Janis

To: Chris
Have you enjoy

VR Janis

Oct 2017

Hidden Memories

ISBN-10: 0984789626
ISBN-13:978-0-9847896-2-7

Hidden Memories

DEDICATION

This book is for my husband and my children who I share great memories with and who help me create memorable events in my life.

Hidden Memories

THE HIDDEN MAGIC TRILOGY

Book 1 – Hidden Powers

Book 2 – Hidden Memories

CONTENTS

Hidden Memories

Hidden Memories

CHAPTER 1

THE HEART of the NATION

Papakoosigun bolted upright in bed, tears and sweat mingling on her face. A scream clenched tightly in her throat. The nightmares were getting worse. She didn't know if they were true dreams or just her fears and worries coming to life. Either way she wanted them to stop.

Mikwam was finished and gone, but the words she threatened two months ago rang through Papakoosigun's head every time she woke up. *You will pay. Do you think I am the only magical creature to feel that way? I have others who will step in my path if I fail. You will have your hands full.*

Papakoosigun called the magic of the sacred token of the Elvin people to banish Mikwam from the elves and take away everything that made Mikwam an elf.

Papakoosigun felt a sort of horror for the changes her magic had created in Mikwam. What if the others she talked about didn't care if the humans knew what they were?

She brushed her deep copper hair out of her face and took a deep breath. She wiped her tears on the blanket and struggled to untangle herself from their twisted threads.

It was time to get up anyway to greet the sun and the new day. She flung back her blanket and felt her way toward the shelf of clothes. She got herself ready and reached out her window until she felt a branch.

Then she climbed the tree next to her window to the top branches and felt the sun reach its first golden rays to touch the town of Big Sur, California and her.

She thought about the sun and about waking up to greet the sun. Like every sunrise before this her thoughts slowly turned to Biboon. A held back cry made her chest ache, but she had no control over the tears streaming down her face.

Biboon had been her teacher, friend, and substitute mother. Papakoosigun ached for the giant and hug her enormous thumb. Biboon had fallen prey to Mikwam over the summer, succumbing to the ice that encased her body. Papakoosigun ran away from the island and Biboon, but now all she wished was to run to Biboon.

She heard her friends arriving in her room, so she turned away from the dawn and slowly climbed out of the tree.

"Ani, guys. Come to check on me again?" Papakoosigun sighed. Her friends checked on her every day, either because of her blindness or more likely because she is the heir to the throne.

"We just wanted to see if you wanted to come to Jean's Haven for some breakfast. It might take your mind off of things." Bagosendam huffed. "It's not like we are going to tell Jean about you climbing the tree, you know she doesn't like it."

Papakoosigun threw up her hands, "I know she doesn't like it, but greeting the sun is a daily ritual I am unwilling to give up. Besides I am not helpless."

"Awibaa, be calm, Papakoosigun. No one said you were."

"I'm sorry," Papakoosigun wore her sorrow like a cloak.

"It's fine. Are you coming?"

"Eya, I am coming." Papakoosigun held out her hand and felt the weight of her jacket. She rubbed her fingers along the fabric, and threw it in the general direction of her bed.

Papakoosigun grinned, "Should we try that again? I can talk slower. I said my jacket not Jean's thick arctic coat. And you say I'm the blind one."

Ishkode laughed and placed her jacket on her shoulders, "Nice try, Bagosendam. I don't think you are ever going to get her."

Papakoosigun started putting her arms in the sleeves as she headed for the door. She heard a distinctive sssshhhh and a whack, she laughed as she waited for Ishkode's arm. Ishkode grabbed her hand

and placed it in the crease of his arm. She was a little confused and turned her head toward him.

Ishkode huffed, "I have to put you on this side, my other arm is sore. A giant punched it with some power."

Papakoosigun laughed again as she pulled Ishkode forward. She kept laughing at her two best friends until they reached the café.

Papakoosigun and her friends were sitting eating their breakfast, when the strangers walked into the little café. The strangers slowly looked through the room as if they were searching for something.

Bagosendam leaned forward to see the strangers better, "Who are they? I wondered what they are here for. It's not tourist season. They seem a little lost, like they are searching for something."

With Bagosendam's words, the two strangers jerked their heads in the direction of their table. They weaved their way through the tables toward them. Ishkode glared daggers at Bagosendam for bringing unwanted attention to them.

One of the strangers was a few inches taller than the other, but in every other way they were similar even down to the way they dressed. The aura they wore like cloaks is what grabbed Papakoosigun's attention. The determination and the success that they found their target radiated from them. These men had aggression and conflict flashing in warning within themselves. This made her want to run away as fast as her legs could carry her.

The strangers halted a few steps away from Papakoosigun's table and bowed deeply at the waist toward Papakoosigun.

"Lady Papakoosigun, we wish to speak with you in private. Daga, please come outside with us."

"What if I don't want to go?"

"Then we will discuss these matters in front of these guests. Let me assure you, you don't want them to hear this."

Papakoosigun huffed, "It seems, I don't have much of a choice. Do I?"

The taller one grinned and bowed again, "Not really, m'lady."

Papakoosigun pushed her chair back and stood. The shorter man gently placed his hand on his arm and walked toward the door. She shook her head slightly when Jean tried to stop them. Ishkode and Bagosendam followed suit. She led them to the community garden. She couldn't explain why, but she didn't want them anywhere near her cabin.

"What is the meaning of this?"

"First, it would please us to introduce ourselves to you, seeing as we will be spending a lot of time together. My name is Bikwak and this is Mitigwaab. We will be your escorts."

Papakoosigun shuddered, "What do you mean about spending a lot of time together? What is going on?"

"M' lady, we have some terrible news. The queen was killed in an accident dealing with humans. She was walking in the forest and some hunters shot her. She named you her heir. You are now our queen."

They bowed again.

"How could something like this happen?"

"It is unknown because the queen was alone, heading toward a meeting with another clan or something. Zhimaagan felt her go. You need to come back to the village with us. Noongom, now. Our people need you."

"I am not ready to go back. When I am ready, I will meet you there."

Bikwak grabbed her arm, "We must insist you come back with us."

Ishkode leaped toward them, tried to disentangled their arms and ended up on his back with Mitigwaab leaning over him. His hands started to glow with fire.

Ishkode voice sounded like liquid fire, deepening by the second, "Please, don't touch her. What right do you have?"

Bikwak sighed, "The council told us to bring her back. We were to decide how to accomplish this. She does not agree, so we will guide her. We don't want trouble."

Papakoosigun struggled against
Bikwak's hold, "Give me just a little time.
You can stay in town and keep an eye on
things. I need a little more . . . apii, time."

"I guess that is acceptable. We will
give you two weeks. We cannot give you
more than that. We are sorry."

Bikwak released her arm and
stepped back.

Papakoosigun's mind spun, she saw
no way out of this. She was going to have to
go the forest elves. The only question was,
how long could she hold off the guards?
Another issue she had to face soon was her
magical token.

At least she didn't feel the pull of the island anymore; she didn't think it was the island to begin with. It was the token, yanking her desires to it. She still felt the pull, but it wasn't toward the island. It was toward the heart of the mainland, where she had hidden the token for safe keeping.

She knew she was going have to go for the token, but the time was questionable. She wanted it with her, but the token stood for everything she didn't want. She didn't want the responsibility of the clan; she wanted to be left alone. If she went for the token it was her saying she was

ready to give up her freedom. She wasn't
ready for that so she resisted the pull.

CHAPTER 2

FRIENDLY SPLASHES

"Jump," Bagosendam demanded of her friend.

"No thanks, but if you are so eager, then be my guest," Papakoosigun held out her hand and bowed to her.

"Jump now or you will be forever labeled the Elvin chicken."

"I am not a chicken and I would not want to take away your title. I made this jump hundreds of times, I just don't want to right now."

"Well, if no one is going to jump I'll push you in and wade to shore alone because you two are giving me a headache," Niibin threatened them, rumbling and grumbling.

The friends lounged on the giant's shoulders goading each other to make the first jump into the ocean. Papakoosigun knew from experience that she had about five seconds before Niibin lost patience. Niibin was not known for his patience.

Biboon tried over and over to teach her son, but it never worked.

Papakoosigun stood raised her arms above her head and winked in her friend's direction. She took a flying leap into the freezing ocean. Her head bobbed above the waves as she waited for friend to hit the water.

"Ha. Ha. Papakoosigun, I win. You jumped in first so I . . . . ."

Niibin shoved Bagosendam into the water with his finger and she flung out her arms to stop herself from falling. Niibin laughed as she hit the water and came up sputtering. He turned and swam toward the island.

Papakoosigun hollered, "Baamaapi, until later, Niibin."

"Race you, Bagosendam," Papakoosigun shouted as she was already swimming toward the mainland.

As their steps raced across the sand toward town, Papakoosigun saw the warriors from the café, Bikwak and Mitigwaab staring at them sternly. They skidded to a halt. Uh-oh.

Papakoosigun counted the days in her head and her fingers. They said two weeks and it had only been eight days. So by her figuring she had six more days.

Papakoosigun muttered under her breath, "What do they want now, to put me in chains?"

Hidden Memories

CHAPTER 3

CHANGES

Bikwak stood with his arms crossed, "Bagosendam, we need to speak to Papakoosigun alone."

Bagosendam glared at them, "You know you should treat her like your queen and not like a child. What is the matter? Did she do something wrong?"

Mitigwaab pointed toward the town and Bagosendam stomped in that direction, "I'm going!"

Papakoosigun plopped down on the beach and dug her feet in the sand. She listened to the sound of the waves as she felt the sun start its descent toward the horizon. She focused on the heat from the sun and ignored the warriors. The scene lost its serenity with Bikwak's next words to Papakoosigun.

"We received a letter today from the elders. You have to leave this place today and go to the village. You need to pack. We will give you until midnight to get ready and say your goodbyes."

Papakoosigun jumped up as if she was scolded with hot water.

"You received a letter about me? Wait. You want me to leave here today? I belong here, this is my home!"

"No, this was never your home; it was just a stopping point in your journey. Your journey must continue now.

"The elders of the elves have requested your presence; I am merely doing what they ask. You are the queen therefore you need to listen to the elders, they advise you on the right choice. Please, giishkowe, stop crying."

"The elders? What do they want from me? Bikwak, why do I have to go? My advisors? They are more like my jailers. I thought you were giving me some time, I still have six days. I belong here with Bagosendam, Ishkode and Jean."

"The elders of the elves have their reasons. You know this is not all of a sudden. Papakoosigun, I told you. I said you would only have a little time. Do you not want to help your people? I gave you as much time as I could."

"I don't want to go. This is my home. What do I have to do to stay? The elders can take care of things without me. I did not ask for this. I don't understand. I did not have enough time. I can't go. I . . . I belong here. Don't I?"

"You belong with the people. I know you don't want to go, but it is for the best. You have to be tired of humans by now. There are rumors that some of the people are panicking since the queen died. I think the elders are hoping you can tame the unease."

Papakoosigun did not understand why it had to be her. Her mind raced with thoughts, tears flooded her eyes as she tilted her head up at the men who had become her shadows.

Bikwak sounded torn, "Oh, Papakoosigun. Don't cry. The elders know the responsibility they ask. All I ask is for you to try. It is all anyone can ask of you. You can come back to visit as soon as everything is settled. The house will always be waiting for you. Jean will too. Now you must get ready. Your escort should be here in the first hour after midnight."

As Papakoosigun tried to talk to Bikwak her words were mumbled together at first. Then suddenly they came bursting out with the anger she could no longer control.

"I know the elders know what they demand. It doesn't matter if it hurts me, as long as I do what is told. All the elders do is demand and I cannot say no! The house will not be mine when I leave! I am banished from the only home I have ever really felt at peace at. It is not fair. I feel it is as much your fault as theirs. You came and found me. You told them you would have me ready when they needed me. I AM NOT READY, and I will never be."

Papakoosigun ran blindly toward her house. Why? Why did she have to listen?

What would happen if she ran away and hid? Would the world end? She slammed the door of the house as she stumbled in.

It was a little one room shack, but it was beautiful. On the window sill she felt the flowers she planted with Jean. She slumped on the twin bed where she slept. Her bed lay in a rumpled mess. She kicked her clothes into a pile on the floor where they were scattered.

Ishkode sat on the edge of her bed, playing with her pillow.

His voice was hesitant, "Papakoosigun?"

"I have to leave." She scooted next to him on the bed, then slid to the floor at Ishkode's feet and laid her head back against his knee. He hugged her briefly then pushed her forward slightly. She felt him pull a brush through her hair. She closed her eyes enjoying the comfort this routine brought her. He sighed.

"Why do you have to leave, now?"

"The elders order it."

He sighed again.

"Let's leave, Papakoosigun. Right now."

Papakoosigun wiped her tears, "Where would we go that they can't find us?"

Ishkode jumped up, "Anywhere, we'll keep moving. Hurry."

Papakoosigun stayed where she was, "Why? They knew I was here. They will find us. I just screamed at Bikwak for doing his job. It didn't fix anything and now I feel guilty."

Ishkode stomped over to her, "Don't give up!"

Papakoosigun shuddered, "I am not giving up. I am giving in. I need to get ready to leave. My escort will be here soon."

Ishkode growled, "If you leave you will never come back. I need you to know . . ."

The door slammed opened and Bagosendam raced in, "So I heard you were leaving tonight. I thought we had days, geez! I was planning a big going away party and everything. We were supposed to go shopping. I don't know what to do now!"

Ishkode growled again, "You could leave!"

Bagosendam ignored him, "Well, I guess we have to get you ready. Why do you always have to be so messy, Papakoosigun? Your hair should be braided for your trip."

Bagosendam finally took a breath, jumped on the bed behind Papakoosigun. She weaved Papakoosigun's hair into a fishbone braid and tied it with a piece of vine. Papakoosigun leaned back again and let the tears flow.

Ishkode huffed and threw up his hands, "Bagosendam, you kind of interrupted an important conversation. Why don't you leave and come back later?"

Bagosendam stuck out her tongue at him, "I want to stay and say good-bye too."

Papakoosigun stood up suddenly, "Bagosendam! Ishkode! I know. Why don't you come with me? Right now."

Ishkode sighed, "Papakoosigun, I want to. Really I do. But I need to finish my orders for the shop and we knew this was coming from the minute they stepped into the café .So I have tried to get it all done. I still have orders to fill. Stop making faces!"

"Must you always follow the rules and orders? It is not fair, I am losing everything and you lose nothing. What if I need you?"

"The elders care for us and we must show the respect due to them. I am losing you. What do you mean? I am losing nothing! I have always and will always be there for you. You know that, don't you? Besides I will be at the village as soon as I can, once I take care of business."

Papakoosigun crossed her arms, "You won't even last three days."

Ishkode grinned, "Stop gloating and go pack."

"Well, act your age and not like an old man. We are only sixteen years and you make me feel old."

He made faces at her and stuck his tongue out.

"There. Is that better? Stop stalling."

Bagosendam stood and pulled Papakoosigun toward her, embraced her tightly then spun her to face the door. Papakoosigun grabbed her pack off the hook hanging on the door and sat it on her bed. Well if she couldn't take Ishkode with her then at least she could hope to talk Bagosendam into going.

"Bagosendam, you didn't answer me earlier. Will you come with me, now?"

"I can't, sorry. I have to help at the island for a little while. Niibin asked me. Once I am done there I will be at the village faster than you can say fairy wishes."

Papakoosigun whispered, "Fairy wishes."

Bagosendam hugged her, "Have a good trip. I will see you, soon. Very soon. I'll miss you. Gotta go, bye."

Bagosendam left as quickly as she came. Papakoosigun placed her books in the bottom of her pack. She hoped she could find someone to read to her like Ishkode normally did. She threw clothes and items all over the room and her bed searching for her carving materials. She guessed she should have just asked Jean, she usually cleans the room.

She placed her carving tools, a few special items, and one extra set of clothes on the books.

She unwrapped the gift she had been working on for the queen to make sure it was fine. She ran her hands over the large shell from the sea carved with the forest over the entire surface. She rewrapped it and then added it as her final item and closed her pack. She would give it to the elders instead. She knew it was necessary to bring a gift for her elders, especially her advisors.

"Okay, I guess I am ready."

She grabbed the bandolier bag she made for her medicines, shouldered her pack and then walked out. She did not look back to envision the how the house looked; she knew it would hurt too much. This little house was not much, but it was hers.

She wanted to hide from everyone, but she knew it was impossible. She went to the beach and sat and waited for midnight.

CHAPTER 4

NIGHT FLIGHT

A green dragon crouched on the beach and watched Papakoosigun through vibrant green eyes. The dragon flashed the colors of the rainbow when it shifted positions and shimmered like the water resting in the sunlight when it was still.

The dragon's aura flashed the same as its skin. She saw the shape of it with the flashes, which made her head hurt a little.

"Ani. Are you to be my escort to the forest elves?"

The dragon thought toward Papakoosigun. *Yes, the elders wanted to stay on the side of safety, therefore I came as order.*

"They are good at giving orders, or so it seems. Why do I need an escort? Why can't I travel on foot with Bikwak and Mitigwaab?"

Don't play dumb, you know you are the queen of the elves now. You need to be protected. Time is moving swiftly, the sooner you are at the village, the better. Shall we go?

"Sure, why not." Papakoosigun shrugged both shoulders into the straps of her pack to a more comfortable location.

Papakoosigun walked to the edge of the water. She climbed on the back of the waiting dragon and straightened her back. She gripped the dragon's body with her legs and grabbed one of the horns growing out of the back of the dragon's head.

She heard a grunt behind her and felt a rope go around her and then felt the weight of someone sitting behind her.

Bikwak laughed, "Sorry, m'lady. It has been a long while since I was on dragon back. Let's be off now. Mitigwaab will meet us there. We flipped a coin and I won the honor of protecting you."

Papakoosigun whispered, "Oh goody for you."

Papakoosigun nodded her head and began the flight toward her new life. She flew toward the new day in the east. She let a few tears escape which drop onto the hide of the dragon.

Do not shed your tears, little one. All will be well.

"I will try not to cry."

Do you want to have some fun while we are flying to the village?

"Fun, what kind of fun? By the way, my name is Papakoosigun."

I know who you are, young one. My name is Zhimaagan; I am the protector of the forest elves. You better hold on.

Bikwak gripped Papakoosigun tighter, "Was Zhimaagan talking about fun? You do know what dragon fun is?"

Papakoosigun sucked in a deep breath and tried to loosen Bikwak's grip, "No."

Bikwak wouldn't let go, "Dragon fun is . . . AH!"

Just as he was going to finish his sentence, Zhimaagan nosed dived. She snapped her wings open just before they hit the ground. She corkscrewed up to the clouds and spiraled down.

Papakoosigun laughed into the wind at Bikwak's holler, feeling the wind snap her braid into Bikwak's face like an angry cat's tail. Bikwak did not loosen his grip. She tried to let Zhimaagan's speed whip away her worries, but her eyes still stung.

Papakoosigun felt like she could reach up and touch the stars, so she lifted her arm up to the wind. Bikwak screeched and grabbed her hand and placed it back on

Zhimaagan's horn. Papakoosigun could not help laughing again, poor Bikwak seemed terrified. She felt no fear because she knew Zhimaagan would protect her.

Zhimaagan continued to do spins, twists and dives through the air as they flew inland. Papakoosigun hung on to the horn in a tight grip; it almost seemed if they were made as hand holds.

Zhimaagan landed in a small meadow. Papakoosigun searched her surroundings, no one was around.

"Why are we stopping here? Are you going to eat me, now, you know play with your food before you eat it?"

Ha. Ha. You're so funny. I would never eat you. Bikwak does not look appetizing with his green coloring.

They both whipped their heads over toward where Bikwak leaning against a tree and taking deep breaths.

I stopped because you have to walk the rest of the way to the village. It is about one mile to the east. I will be behind you, but you must walk in front.

"Why?"

You are important and need to be seen by all. The elders know we are close and on our way. We must continue on, we cannot keep them waiting.

Papakoosigun trudge at a slow pace, but Zhimaagan did not lose patience with her.

Why do you drag your feet, little one? You will get there one way or another.

"I don't know what to do when I meet the elders. What if I make a mistake?"

You are the queen. All you have to do is remember the training of your teachers. If you make a mistake, it will be forgiven. We all know you have been gone a long time.

"How do you know me and how long I have been gone? Where have I been gone from? I have always lived on my island and in Big Sur."

You left here as a tiny girl to live on the island. This village is where you were born. We are there.

CHAPTER 5

ROYAL TREATMENT

Papakoosigun slipped through thick, tall bushes into a large meadow with a massive tree in the middle. They reached the village at the same time the new sun touched the tops of the surrounding trees.

Standing in front of the massive tree was a line of elders.

Papakoosigun glided to the elders and as she did the clearing filled with people. Cheering started quietly and built up to a roar by the time she stood in front of the elders. The elders knelt on one knee and bowed to her and the rest of the people followed suit.

One of the elders cleared her throat quietly before she spoke.

"Please be welcome, my queen. We are happy to have you home at last. This is a great day for our people and a new beginning for you. My name is Nenookaasi; I am the speaker of the elders."

"It is my duty to do the bidding of the people. I would like to present this gift on behalf of the residents of the Forgotten Island." Papakoosigun refused to meet the elders' eyes.

Papakoosigun felt the elders bow to the people. She followed their lead and bowed also. Nenookaasi spoke loudly so the people around them could hear her.

"We will retire to the dining room. There is much to discuss with our queen."

Nenookaasi waved to the villagers then turned and walked into the massive tree behind her. Papakoosigun's head turned toward the flashes that she knew were Zhimaagan. Zhimaagan nodded her head and then curled up and watched the people. Papakoosigun followed the elders reluctantly.

They walked into a hallway with rooms branching off at regular intervals. At the end of the hall was the dining room. An enormous table took up most of the room, surrounded by beautifully craved chairs.

Papakoosigun ran her hand along the carving admiring the clean sweep of the forest leaves playing across the surface. She noticed a small repeating pattern; it was the signature mark of the carver. The master carver who worked on the chair was Rosha and belongs to the grizzly bear clan of dwarves. Rosha! It could not be.

He was the master carver who taught her. He laughed at her first pieces, but he was a great teacher. The first pieces she carved looked like hazy clouds in the sky when they were meant to be leaves dancing on vines. The thought made her smile. She felt everyone was staring at her, expecting. Apparently, someone asked her something.

Their eyes followed her around the room as she walked around the table.

Nenookaasi sat at the left side of the head of the table. Nenookaasi's aura was flowing with calm colors. The chair at the head of the table was empty, waiting for her. Most of the people around the table were elders of the clans, with the exception of one, a young man to the right of her chair.

Papakoosigun studied the occupants of the room intuitively as she walked toward her chair. Her eyes wandered to the chair beside hers. Nenookaasi waved her hand in this person's direction, "This young man is our new cave ambassador is Aki."

Papakoosigun studied his color; she knew without the subtle shift in starlight colors on the edge of his aura she would not have noticed him. His entire being was the black of complete stillness. He seemed very mysterious.

Her eyes drifted to the next person and she gasped in wonder. Beside Aki was unique creature and Papakoosigun was surprised she ventured out of her environment. Her coloring flashed the colors of the ocean and moving water. It was in constant motion. Nenookaasi spoke quietly, "This is our water ambassador, Ziibi."

There was woman on the side of Nenookaasi. Her colors flashed from white to pale blue. Papakoosigun felt the cold coming off the woman from her spot. She was glad she was not sitting next to her. Nenookaasi gestured to the woman, "This is our ice ambassador, Dakaagamin."

Heat was radiating out of the man next to Daakaagamin. He had colors that shifted first red, orange, yellow. The movement of the colors was stiff which showed his discomfort. "This man is the fire ambassador, Waawaatesi."

Nenookaasi sighed, "Our desert ambassador, Bingwi is a little impatient for the introductions to be over. He has had a long journey and is tired."

Bingwi voice was deep and gravelly, "I do not need you to explain for me. We are all tired it has been a long few weeks." His colors yellows and flashed with irritation for talking and being in the room.

Next to Bingwi was a woman whose colors flowed in a peaceful circle. Her voice flowed too. "And I am the mountain ambassador, Aanakwad. Now that is everyone here. Please, sit down,

Papakoosigun. I am sorry; I feel sometimes it is tiring to have a speaker for all of us."

Papakoosigun sat down on the edge of her seat. She gripped the armrest tightly and then slowly eased back. Why was everyone still staring at her?

Nenookaasi sighed, "It is truly great to have you back with us, Papakoosigun."

"I am glad to be of service." She could not say she was glad to be back, everyone would know it was a lie.

Nenookaasi reached over and grabbed her hand, "I know you are confused, so I will explain. The queen announced to us and then the people that you were her niece and she named you her heir. Then a week later, she went out to speak to the magical creatures that do not live near our village. She was walking through a field and was shot through the heart by a hunter.

"We feel great pain at losing a wonderful leader, but we need to move on. You are the leader of the people now. We are here to guide you. The people were panicked when we lost the queen. Now that you are here everything will fall into order."

"No, I am not your queen. I am a young girl who grew up on an island with my twin. Surrounded by people who took me in and taught me all I know."

"They raised you and your brother on the queen's orders. They taught you what she wanted you to learn. We could trust you and your brother to the training they provided you. We know it is a lot to take in and hard to adjust, but you will learn to love it here."

"What if I don't want to be here? Do I have a choice?"

Nenookaasi stared hard at her, "Your majesty, it is hard to believe you would put yourself and your wants before the people."

"I will not be selfish."

"We are glad you are here for the people."

"If you are the ambassadors of the clans of elves why are you the only ones? Biboon taught me there is a clan of elves for every environment and element on Gashi Aki. Why are there not more?"

"Some of the clans decide to hide from the humans in their own way and isolated. That is their choice. You will stay here and learn to stand for the forest elves. We have a lot of issues to deal with this year. The humans continue to move into our forest and clear cut. We need to find a solution to this problem. ”

"I will try and make the best of the situation. It was the way I was raised."

"We need you to figure out how we can work with humans or how we can best avoid them. The barrier you put around the village has helped us a great deal, but it doesn't save the forest further out. It is distressing. Zhimaagan wants to see you as soon as you're settled this evening."

Papakoosigun stood, "Why can't I see Zhimaagan now?"

Nenookaakosi laughed, You are going to be very busy this morning. We are going to have a celebration in the clearing this morning."

"It is necessary? I was hoping to see my room and refresh myself before any festivals or gatherings took place."

"I am sorry, but as leaders we need to listen to the needs of the people. They anticipate a celebration now that our new queen has arrived. Zhimaagan will be in the clearing, as guardian of the people."

"Whatever you wish."

"Thank you, your majesty."

CHAPTER 6

SADDEN CELEBRATION

Papakoosigun picked at her food feeling like a child being punished.

Nenookaasi pushed her chair back. "It is time we join the people. Please, your majesty follow me."

As they step outside, Nenookaasi spoke softly, "All of the people worked to decorate the meadow to welcome you. The streamers and ribbons look beautiful blowing on the breeze. The prayer ties are for you to have a good, long, healthy life to help the people. Everyone is dressed in their finest."

"How could so much change happen while we ate? We were not gone long. Do you think I should go change out of my traveling outfit?"

"The people worked hard to please you. You are dressed fine, for now. Maybe Aki can show you around."

The people surrounded and pulled all of them into a round dance. The male ambassadors danced with all of the female ambassadors, switching partners with each song.

As Papakoosigun danced with Aki, he seemed to think he needed to try to be polite.

"My lady, was the trip good?"

"Yes."

"Are you enjoying the forest?"

"Yes."

"Is there anything you need?"

"No."

"Can you give any answers besides one word?"

"No." Papakoosigun fought not to smile.

"Great."

"What is great?"

"Ah, she can speak. See I can speak one word at a time, too."

"Ha. Ha. You're so funny. Quiet now, I am thinking."

To her surprise he grew quiet and then someone else cut in.

Finally late evening, the elders declared it was time to retire.

"Before we retire for the evening, I would like to announce that we will meet in the morning at the meeting hall to discuss some issues for the realm. Good night to all of you."

A dwarf elder came up to Papakoosigun. She only came up to Papakoosigun's waist. She wore a long cloak covering most of her features, but her face was beautiful. She looked like a short, stocky elf, but instead of her features being sharp they were more rounded and warm. She had a motherly feel to her.

"I am Ahsin. I am your personal helper and caretaker. I will show you to your room, if you are ready."

Papakoosigun jumped to the side of Ahsin.

"Yes, I am more than ready. I want to get settled and relax."

Papakoosigun stepped through the door of her room. White curtains framed a door in the opposite wall, which opened on to a balcony. The door was opened all the way, letting in the night. There was a massive bed filling one of the remaining walls. Two bedside tables were squeezed between the bed and the walls. The other

71

wall held doors as well. Papakoosigun walked to these wondering what was on the other side.

"These doors lead to your closet. I took the liberty to acquire you dresses in your clan colors. There is a washing basin in there as well. Your majesty, there are dark circles under your eyes, and your skin looks pale. I think you should rest. Would you like me to close the door to the balcony?"

"No, please keep the door open. It is really hot in here."

"Is there anything else you need?"

"No, I am fine. Thank you."

"I will be in the next room if you need me."

"Thank you, again."

Papakoosigun took her pack off her shoulder, and dug until she came up with her brush. She sadly undid the braid Bagosendam had patiently done. It was silly, but the braid felt like her last tie to her friends and she did not want to lose it. She pulled the brush through her hair until it shined.

"I hoped I make you proud of me, my friends."

Papakoosigun did not like her hair down most of the time so she whipped her hair up and twisted it, securing it with a stick from her bag. She used water from the basin and washed her face and rubbed some into her neck.

She heard a flutter of wings and heard a bird land on her bedside table. The bird waited patiently for her to respond.

"Where did you come from, biineshiinh? You smell like you came from the shore, a little of the sea and sands. But you wouldn't fly this far from home. Would you?"

She ran her fingers over him and felt him raise his leg. Then she felt the small tube tied to it.

"What do you have there? Is that for me? Thank you."

She reached over and untied the tube and shook out the contents in her hand. He sat still, waiting. In her hand she felt a small shell and a roll piece paper. She placed the shell on the table and unrolled the paper with shaking hands.

"Ahsin! Please come here."

Ahsin came running in, "What is it? Is something wrong, our majesty?"

"I need your help to read this. Please."

"With pleasure. Do you want to know who it is from first?"

"Yes, that would be nice."

"It says it is from Bagosendam."

Her heart soared. Then she sat hard on the bed and felt the separation more keenly.

Ahsin placed a hand on her shoulder, "You alright?"

Papakoosigun struggled to get the word passed the lump in her throat, "Yes."

Day 1

Papakoosigun,

I wrote day 1 because it is the first day we are apart. I miss you; it feels as if I am missing my favorite pair of socks or an arm. The shell is a little piece of home to hold you steady. I hope it helps. Jean says the house seems empty without you and your tricks. Ishkode has no time for me he is rushing to get done with his work. He says to tell you he misses you and he will be there soon.

Sleep well, my friend. Bagosendam

"The bird is still waiting, your majesty. Do you want to send a letter back? I can write it for you. Whatever you say will be kept in secret."

"What can I say to her? I am overjoyed by knowing I am stuck here. Yeah right. But I cannot sound unhappy, they are worried enough. So cheerful it is. I can do this. Okay, Ahsin I think I am ready."

"Please wait one second, m'lady. I know there is paper and pen here in one of these drawers. Oh, here it is. Alright, I am ready to begin."

Hidden Memories

Bagosendam,

I miss you dearly. I am thankful for my little piece of home. I will make it into a necklace so I can carry it with me always. I am happy I came if only to sit in the trees and listen to the wind in the leaves. It smells different here, more like the earth and less like the sea. I am sorry the house does not seem the same. I feel a piece of me is missing too, but I am not going to compare you to a pair of socks. You are my steady rock always pushing me back on the path I have to walk. I love you like a sister. I will dream of home and of all of you. Tell Jean I miss her and her muffins. Tell Ishkode I am waiting. I am waiting for you, too. Papakoosigun

Ahsin laughed, "Sorry, m'lady. It is just the socks part was funny."

Papakoosigun let herself have a small smile, "It was. Bagosendam has an interesting sense of humor. Can you hand it to me?"

"Yes, here m'lady. Will there be anything else?"

"No, I think I just need to be alone for a little while. Miigwech for the help."

"It was my pleasure, m'lady. Do not hesitate to call me again if you need anything."

Papakoosigun sighed, "I will."

With a heavy heart she put her letter in the tube. She wished she could fit in there too. She heard the bird flutter its wings and soar out of the doorway. She cleaned up, for something to do. Jean always cleaned up her carvings and mess. It made her miss home all the more.

The night was better even if tomorrow was unknown. It was better because rain was falling. If she could not have the sound of the ocean then the rain was better than the quiet. It was a heavy rain, the kind that drowned out all other sounds.

She listened to the booming of the thunder. She still could not go to sleep even though the rain was soothing. She was thinking of home. She was thinking of the meeting tomorrow. Tears escaped, even though she was fighting to hold them in.

Papakoosigun climbed under the covers and laid her head on one of the many pillows on the bed. She closed her eyes and sighed drifting off to sleep.

CHAPTER 7

REALITY

She woke up, greeted the sun and then decided to go enjoy the weather. She went for a walk along the lake next to the village. She slowly drifted back to the village when she heard a waterfall. She stopped to listen to it and the birds singing when she heard people calling her name. It was time to go back.

The elders were waiting for her when she returned. Their colors were muted and blank; Papakoosigun could not read anything from them.

"Where were you, this morning? Your caretaker came to help you and you were gone."

"I went for a walk."

"You know the duty you have to the people. Yet you do not seem to understand. You were supposed to be at the meeting. You are blind and should not be wandering around alone. We cannot have anything happen to you. What do you have to say for yourself?"

Papakoosigun sighed, "I didn't think I was gone so long."

Nenookaasi fumed, "That is right, you didn't think. . . hmmm. But that is neither here nor there. We can think of nothing else to do. We are sorry it has come to this."

The elders stood in a circle around her. She saw their auras shifting into each other and swirling faster and faster. She could not pull away or move. When the elders moved away, she felt no different.

"What did you do to me?"

"You cannot leave the area of the village unless one of us gives you permission. We will see how you are in two weeks time."

"You cannot do this to me."

"We already did and it is for your own safety. You will go change for the meal; a dress is laid out for you."

How could they? Papakoosigun went up to her room and put on a dark green dress, twisted up her hair in a stick and went down. She wanted to go test this limit they placed on her, maybe later tonight. She walked in and was shocked to see all of the chairs filled except for hers.

The meal was slow, slower for Papakoosigun than for the rest because she did not want to be there. She did not look up from the meal, but got the feeling people were staring at her.

Finally, dessert was carried away. She waited. She had to wait at least ten minutes for it to be polite to leave the table. The minutes dragged by. As she was about to stand, Nenookaasi cleared her throat.

"Thank you all for coming. It is a great occasion for our young queen to be here after so long.

"We have two pieces of important news. First, we have to go investigate the western shores of this continent. Unfortunately, the queen will have to go with one or two of us.

"There have been reports of plants growing quickly and crushing buildings. It needs to be taken care of. The second piece of news is the elders have decided the young queen's betrothed as of today."

"The union is of our queen Papakoosigun to Aki. This union will be one to remember. He was chosen as the best match. The union will take place ...." That was all Papakoosigun heard and then a roar began in her ears. What was going on?

Papakoosigun could feel the anger and tears rising up in her, she tried to maintain control. Aki reached over and grabbed her hand. She flinched away, but he still held her hand. Did he think this was okay?

LET GO! She screamed at him in her thoughts. He let go quickly and almost fell back in his chair. She thought everyone in the room heard her yell, but she was beyond caring. She jumped up from her seat knocking the chair to the ground. His touch had pushed her control over the edge.

"I will not be joined to this man. He is not my choice. I came here for you, but I did not forfeit my life to you. No! No! I will not do this!"

Nenookaasi held her arms out, "Calm down. I said. Calm down! Yes, you will, it is your *Duty*. It is time to face reality and your responsibilities."

"It is all about *Duty* with you people. I will not do this!" Papakoosigun stormed out of the room and was upstairs in seconds, using her speed to help her escape. She slammed her door and then went to the balcony. She climbed to the top of the trees, for once cursing her Elvin ears. She could feel most of the guests leave and she could hear everything they said.

The elders had a reassuring tone, "Not to worry, the young queen will come around. It is her duty and she will do it."

How could the elders do this to her? Wasn't it enough to come back here? Under orders, no less. First the elders bind her to the village and now they are trying to marry her off. The tears would not stop, no matter how deep of breaths she took. She wanted to disappear.

She went down to her room when the sky was pitch black. Not a star in the heavens. The sky was filled with dark angry purple clouds. Maybe the sky was reading her mood. A storm was fast approaching.

She closed the balcony doors. Papakoosigun curled up on the floor next to her bed with a blanket and cried until there was nothing left. She sighed and went to the closet. She washed her face and dressed in her favorite pants and shirts. Papakoosigun went to the edge of the village and tried to walk toward the waterfall. She could not take one step into the trees.

She dragged her feet as she went back to her room. It was not her fault, but she could not help feeling guilty for getting angry. Papakoosigun's room already felt like the safest place in the village. The elders never went up to her room. She went to the bed and curled up in a ball hoping sleep would take her away from *duty* for awhile.

She gasped as she woke from a dream of vines squeezing the breath out of her. She jumped up, dressed, strapped on her sword and snatched her bow from the side table. She would have to thank Ishkode for sending it with Mitigwaab.

She headed to the docks in the morning to enjoy the water and fresh air. Aki came to see her, but Bikwak and Mitigwaab stopped him before he got close. It was the first time she was happy they were always close. Aki did not leave though;

he sat at another dock and watched them with a frustrated look. He tried to talk to her a couple of times, but Ahsin stopped him.

Papakoosigun, will you not talk with me?

No! She would not listen to his thoughts or his words. He stood up.

She stood up as well and walked around the village hoping for a miracle to help her. She wanted to leave, but with the spell she had no chance. It was as if Zhimaagan read her thoughts, which she considered a possibility. Zhimaagan stood and snapped opened her wings.

It is time to go investigate the shore, little one.

Papakoosigun was happy for the first time since the news. Bikwak was behind her and then Aki walked up.

Zhimaagan sat waiting. *I can only carry three, little one. This is going to be a long tiring flight so you have to behave. Do you understand?*

Papakoosigun took a step closer to Bikwak, so that he blocked Aki from sight, "I can behave as long as he doesn't touch me."

Bikwak bowed, "I promise, he will not touch you."

They climbed on, first Papakoosigun, then Bikwak and finally Aki. Bikwak tied them all in and Zhimaagan spread her wings.

Bikwak gripped Papakoosigun tightly as he spoke, "Zhimaagan, do you promise no spins, twists or dives?"

Zhimaagan lifted off the ground with a roar that slowly turned into her gruff laugh. It did not go unnoticed that she did not promise. Even without the promise, the flight was uneventful. They landed outside of Big Sur.

Papakoosigun looked around, "Is this a joke?"

Aki searched the area, "No joke, this is where most of the activity was reported."

They walked along the edge of town, noticing it was where most of the damage was. Papakoosigun could feel plants growing.

"Most of the growth has happened very quickly and then left to nature. It is moving in slow circles, moving closer to town."

Papakoosigun sat on the ground and concentrated on the growth of the plants in the area. All of the sudden, she jumped up from the ground and ran closer to town.

"I feel the rapid growth happening now! Whoever is doing this is here now! Hurry!"

As Papakoosigun ran she knew where she would end up. She felt the plants grow around her cabin and slowly crush it to nothing.

Papakoosigun heard Jean come running from town and then scream. Papakoosigun ran closer and then fell on her face as vines reached out and tripped her. She tried to call on her power as a forest elf to make the growth normal again. Nothing she did worked.

There was only one person she knew that was stronger in growing power than she was. But it couldn't be him, could it?

"Sorry sister, are you hurt?"

"Opichi? What are you doing?"

"Only a little justice sister."

Papakoosigun was struggling to get free when she faltered in shock of the pain in Jean scream.

"Stop it! Stop it, Opichi! Now!"

"No, I don't think I will."

"Why? I don't understand."

"You wouldn't, sister. What was between us is gone. You may be my twin, but you don't know me."

Papakoosigun wiggled her arms free, kneeled on the ground and grabbed her bow off her back, notching an arrow.

She shot the arrow toward Jean and severed the vine that she felt creeping up around Jean's neck. Papakoosigun could feel Jean's fear as she loaded another arrow.

Jena gasped and passed out as a crack echoed through the area. Papakoosigun turned her arrow toward her brother.

"Why, Opichi?"

"While Mikwam was on the island waiting for you and trying to find the token, we talked. She knew who I was. You didn't even look for me. I am tired of hiding on the island. I have been alone."

"Still, why hurt Jean?'

"Jean, Jean! You care for her, that's why. I was going to kill her, but I had a better idea. A last minute idea. If I can't walk without assistance, neither should she."

You selfish, poisonous asabikeshiinh!"

Opichi shuffled closer toward her, leaning heavily on a cane.

"Don't worry it will only hurt a little."

A vine crept over and wrapped around her chest yanking her to the ground. She had more control over it with it touching the skin of her arms and was able to make it loosen its grip. She sliced it with her sword. She glared in the direction of her brother.

"That was a mistake, brother. Do you think you have been the only one to suffer?"

She stalked over to him. Her hands reached out and grasped his. She smelled the fear pouring off of him. She let the token do what it would.

It softened the punishment because he was her brother. He could grow flowers, grass and small trees, but nothing else. He would have the urge to fill all of the barren spots he saw. He would help the earth repair itself. She felt all of this as she held him.

Papakoosigun released him and slumped to the ground unconscious. The last thing she heard was a roar, a ripping sound and sirens.

She did not remember the flight back and woke in her bed. She felt so weak, even her eyes felt heavy. She closed them wishing for sleep.

Ahsin walked into the room and opened the drapes over the balcony doors.

"I know you are awake, m'lady. I think after the whole day in bed you would want to get up."

"Not really."

"Too bad."

"How is Jean?"

"She will live, but he accomplished his goal. She will never walk again. She is in the hospital now."

"Can I see her?"

"No, not yet anyway. Now, I need you up and eating. Let's go downstairs and see what we can find."

"What about Opichi?"

"He is on the island and weak. I hope he stays there, personally. No offense. Hurry, let's go."

Ahsin guided her into the sitting room of the house. Ahsin wanted to go over the schedule for tomorrow and make sure Papakoosigun did not mess it up. They walked in while the elders were meeting with Aki. His voice was raised, but still held respect in it as he addressed the elders.

"I would like the opportunity to talk to Papakoosigun alone. Get to know her. Make sure this arrangement will work out."

"You cannot talk to her alone; it would be disrespectful and inappropriate. The arrangement will go through as planned, do not worry about that."

"I would still like to speak with her, it would not be inappropriate if we had an escort."

"We will think on it; that is all we can promise. The union was decided for the best. Now, we have issues to attain to."

Papakoosigun could hear the dismissal in Nenookaasi's voice.

"Thank you." Apparently he could, too.

Papakoosigun did not know how to feel about them talking about her in this way. It felt wrong as if she were a pet about to change hands. She wanted to scream some more, but she knew that it wasn't going to help. So instead she walked pass the room into the dining room.

Aki passed her in the hall and she felt his eyes on her, but she did not look up. She made a plate, but then could not bring herself to sit down.

"I don't want to have a union with anyone." Papakoosigun said the words through clenched teeth and she stomped up the stairs to her room.

Papakoosigun listened to Ahsin reading the poetry book Ishkode gave her. It was fun to lose herself in the writing of another person.

Long ago, in an unknown place,

She sat and waited and watched,

Listening to the world fill her space.

Watching the rushing water pushing

pass rocks on its way to its destination.

Sounds like voices speaking in a

language she cannot understand.

Straining to grasp any meaning of

the noises around her.

Feeling the touch that belonged to

none.

The spirits are trying to feel their

space with meaning.

Long ago, in an unknown place,

She sat and waited and watched,

Listening to the world fill her space.

She fell asleep and dreamt of seeing

people around her, but not being seen,

heard or felt. She was the ghost. She saw

someone looking at her and then he looked

into her eyes and she woke up with a start.

With her eyes opened she could make out fuzzy shapes around the room. Maybe her eyesight was coming back. Maybe that was too much to ask for.

Papakoosigun walked into the dining room. Aki was sitting beside Papakoosigun's chair *again*. She sat down quietly and looked at the table.

"Now, I get to see you again, Papakoosigun." She never noticed before, but his voice was warm and musical.

"Yes." She tried to be nice. Maybe they could be friends. She would try for that *at least*.

Nenookaasi interrupted with a question Papakoosigun was hoping she would not ask. "What are you going to do today?"

"Umm. I was thinking of hiding in my room."

Nenookaasi was going to say something else, but an Elvin lad came in and walked briskly toward her. He leaned toward her and whispered. She stood quickly and glided toward the door, the other elders followed quickly after her.

"I am sorry to you all, but a matter has come up. We need to see to it personally. Enjoy your meal."

Aki and everyone else in the room seem to relax as soon as the elders exited. Papakoosigun relaxed as well, leaning back into her chair. She ate her wild rice slow. Most of the guests excused themselves when the elders left. That was fine with her, there was only one problem. Aki, Ahsin and she were the only ones left.

Aki angled his whole body toward Papakoosigun. Great. She grabbed some of the homemade bread in front of her and stood up.

"Please, will you stay and talk with me?"

"Is there a point?"

"The point is to get to know one another."

"I think I should retire to my rooms."

He sat very still, only moving to incline his head. She felt guilty.

She walked to the entrance of the dining room and had a second thought. She turned back toward Aki.

"I hope you enjoy this morning, Aki." She smiled, the elders would like this.

Ahsin followed her to her room.

"Did you enjoy breakfast?"

"Yes, I did. Ahsin, what do you think of Aki?"

"I think he is a nice boy. He has been thrown in this as surely as you have. I am glad you were nice this morning. I am having a hard time with the elders' announcement as well."

"You are having a hard time?"

"You can deal with this and the elders." Ahsin laughed loudly, "Don't make such faces. You will be fine and I will be beside you the entire time. Remember what you are named for Papakoosigun, the willow always bends, but never breaks."

"I think I will try to be friends. I cannot try for anything else. As the elders said I need to face reality and grow up."

"That's the way of it."

CHAPTER 8

PROTECTOR

While Papakoosigun was confined in the village she did some carving. She carved herself a flute and was playing it in her room as rain poured down outside. Ziibi was curled on her bed. Ziibi sighed softly, "I miss the water! Hearing the rain only makes it worse."

Papakoosigun jumped up and grabbed Ziibi's hand and dragged her out onto the balcony and jumped to the ground. They ran into the clearing and danced and spun in the rain. They were enjoying the feel of the drops on their faces, dancing faster and faster until they fell over dizzy and laughing.

"Ziibi, can we go see the waterfall? I want to leave the village. You are an elder, and the only one who doesn't act like a stuffy old coot."

"I guess I should thank you for not thinking I am stuffy, old or a coot. But. . ."

"Oh, please no buts."

"The restriction is in place for a reason. You have to be protected, we cannot afford to lose you."

"Don't you want to see the water, not just rain, but the waterfall? We can go and be back before anyone knows it."

"That is not fair, you know my weakness and you use it against me."

"That is not what I was trying to do. I just know that you need to get away from here as much as I do."

"Fine, you are right and you win. We can go if you promise that we come back in about an hour. I may be one of the elders, but I don't want to be the lone one going against all the rest."

Papakoosigun grabbed her pack. When they reached the barrier, Papakoosigun grabbed hold of Ziibi's hand and let her lead her through.

"One good thing, Ziibi. We know with the rain coming down how it is we won't see anyone. We are the only two people crazy enough to come out in a rain storm."

Ziibi yanked her down into a crouch and whispered, "You spoke too soon. There is someone else out here. I hear them and smell the smoke from their fire. I knew I

117

should not have taken you out of the village."

Papakoosigun huffed, "I think it was a great idea, now we can see who is traipsing around the forest so close to the village. I am not going to go back, so please don't even ask. Let's get a closer look."

Papakoosigun crept slowly closer to the smell of the fire. She could make out the shape of a young boy with a baby resting in a cradleboard strapped to his back. The sky was darkening so he started to set up camp in a hollowed out tree. He always kept the baby against the tree and his back to her, looking out into the forest. He shifted nervously every few minutes.

The boy scraped out all the old rotting needles and gathered some fresh branches to lie down. He fixed up their bed and then placed the fish wrapped in leaves in the fire. He let the baby out and she crawled into his lap while the fish cooked.

"We have been alone for months now maybe close to a year, but it's okay. Everything will be okay. I don't mind taking care of you, little sister."

"Brother."

"Do you know our mother is a spirit now who watches over where ever we go?"

His little sister shook her head like she did every night.

"Yes, she is. She guards us while we sleep. When you were six months old, mother got really sick. Father went to get help and never came back. Mother became a spirit. I promised mother I would always watch over you and take care of you. Did you know today is my day of birth? I am nine years old now."

The baby clapped her hands. They ate the fish and curled up together. She fell asleep quickly.

"I bet you are tired after all the walking today. You are getting stronger. You walked further today then you did yesterday. You look more like our mother than I do. I love you, Wigwaasi."

Ziibi described the baby for Papakoosigun, "She has tan skin, deep brown eyes that had circles in them like the core of a tree. Now they are closed because she is sleeping in her brother's arms. She has long chestnut brown hair that is braided."

"What does the boy look like?"

"He has light skin, blond curly hair that is in the middle of his back. His hair is

121

braided too, but you can see curls coming out everywhere. He has the same deep brown eyes as the baby. What are we going to do?"

"Wait we do not want to startle him. It is dark. If we go back now, we could lose him. We keep watch. I'll take first watch."

Ziibi slept curled up next to her and she watched for movement. He let the fire burn low, but kept it going so Wigwaasi wouldn't get cold. He drifted to sleep holding her. He was startled awake by grunting and snuffling near his head. She shoved Ziibi to wake her.

He slowly dragged his sister closer to himself and then climbed over her. As he shifted a twig snapped. The snuffling stopped and then a ROAR filled the night air.

He grabbed his knife and slashed at the shadow that blocked out the moonlight.

"I don't want to hurt you. Agwas! Go Away!"

He stepped closer to the shadow and led it further from his sister. The shadow roared and swiped at him and hit him in the arm. Blood ran down his arm. Tears ran down his face. Shakes ran down his body. The boy hollered and made a great slash with his knife. He felt it contact with the shadow and heard a grunting roar. The shadow turned and ran. In the moonlight Papakoosigun saw it was a young bear.

He lay down next to his sister. He comforted her and then passed out. He woke as a shadow fell over his face.

Papakoosigun leaned over him. He whipped out his knife and climbed over his sister so she was up against his back.

"I am not going to hurt you, young warrior. I just saw your fire and came to investigate. I did not like a fire so close to my home. As I got near I heard a little crying. Are you okay? You are bleeding. Let me help you. Would you like to come meet my friends?"

"How do I know I can trust you?"

"I am an elf like you."

"That is no reason to give you blind faith."

"True. I am glad you are so cautious. If you want I can bring my friends to meet you."

"I may not be here when you come back."

"Maybe not, but I think my friends would like to meet you."

"I will put my sister in her cradleboard, and then I will come with you. I will not go into any house though."

Papakoosigun wanted to bind the boy's arm, but he would let her. So she led the young boy through the woods until they were near the village. Then she saw a young girl climb down from a tree.

"Papakoosigun, there you are! I just got here, this morning. The elders were wondering where you were. What . . ."

She skidded to a halt in front of them and blushed.

"Bagosendam, these are some friends I found along my way home. I thought you might want to meet them. The healers might want to meet them too. Don't you think so?"

"Hello. I thought you said friends. I see only one."

The little boy reached behind his back and pulled his sister into view.

"Oh."

"Hello. I am glad the princess has brought me to meet you."

She gasped.

"I don't know what you mean. She is not a princess and we don't like nicknames."

"It is not a nickname. I know who she is. She is the blinded princess. My parents told me stories about all of you and Mikwam. My mother described you and told me to be wary of strangers."

"It seems there can be no secrets with this young man. Bagosendam, why don't you go get a healer. This young man does not want to go into any houses."

Papakoosigun turned back toward him and heard Ziibii cooing to the baby behind him. The boy relaxed as soon as he heard her admit to being who he thought.

"I am fine now. I know we are safe. My mother trusted you and I will follow her example." He bowed to her. She smiled and inclined her head.

"My mother told me if there was one person in the world she trusted above all others, it was you Papakoosigun."

"Who was your mother?"

"You knew her from the Forgotten Island, her name was Mitig."

"I remember all the mischief we caused together. Then one day I woke and she was gone. What happened to her?"

"She was ordered to the forest by the queen. She fell in love and had a union with our father. They left the village and lived on their own. She grew sick and he went for help. He never came back. She said you had a secret word, can you tell me what it was?"

"Mishiiminag, apples. No one on the island understood why when we were around each other or passed each other we would say it. It made it all the more funnier, we use to take apples from the cellar. Your mother didn't have a sweet tooth, she had an apple tooth."

A tear slid down her face, "I am so sorry to hear she is gone and that you are alone. I am guessing your name is Soongede'e and your little sister's name is Wigwaasi. Your mother said that she was going to have two babies and she already had their names picked out. She said it was destiny. You don't have to be alone anymore I would love it if you would stay with us. We can take care of each other."

"I would like that."

He walked over to Papakoosigun and she put her arm around him. She ripped a piece off her skirt and bounded his arm tightly. She led him up to the tree. When she got to the door she grinned, there waiting leaning against the wall was Ishkode.

"I will take your sister. You are hurt and weak from losing blood." Papakoosigun grabbed the cradleboard and walked into the house and started to climb the stairs. He swiftly followed, with Ishkode bringing up the rear. At the top of the stairs she turned.

"Ziibi, can you tell the elders I will meet with them later. I want to get these two settled. Bagosendam should be back with the healer at any minute. They need

some protection and I am the one to do it.
Thank you for everything, Ziibi."

Papakoosigun turned toward
Ishkode, "I am so glad you are here. Maybe
you can help find Soongede'e something to
wear. We can talk later."

"It's a deal, and I will get right on
that."

CHAPTER 9

RICING

Papakoosigun kneeled in the back of
her canoe, waiting for the boat to glide
closer to the rice beds. She watched Ishkode
out of the corner of her eye. She was
supposed to be gathering rice with Aki, but
she dove into Ishkode's canoe, ducking and

hiding until he pulled far away from the shore.

He leaned into the pole, bending to bring the canoe deeper into the lake. He stood and placed the pole ahead of the canoe and bent to move the canoe once more. He felt her eyes on him and turned to study her.

"Hey. How can you look peaceful and relaxed? Are you just hiding your anxiousness about your ceremony later today? I am nervous as a mukwa trying to get honey from the bees."

She laughed at the image of a nervous bear being chased by bees. Yes, she was nervous about the ceremony, but not scared. The smile stayed on her face as she thought about becoming a leader of the people. She thought about being in the village, and knowing this part didn't bother her anymore.

She knocked rice into the canoe in a rhythm, making a beat every time her knocking sticks struck together.

Ishkode cleared his throat, "So are you going to tell me about the hide and seek you were trying to do earlier?"

"I just didn't want to see the elders, *any* of the elders. Well, besides Ziibii anyway."

"I heard about you being confined to the village. Which makes me wonder how you got out to find Soongede'e. "

"Can I keep no secrets from you?"

"No. And it seems you are not very good at hiding. Soongede'e is watching the canoe. His staring has drawn the attention of the elders. One young one in particular. Care to explain what happened while I was gone?"

"No."

After their canoe was filled with the rice she knocked in, Ishkode turned their birchbark canoe toward the shore. It took them only a couple of hours of the last day of a long week of ricing. Since no one went out twice in one day, she would be given time to get ready.

She stepped out when the canoe grazed the shore and helped to pull it out of the water. She felt all the busy activity of all members of the clan participating in processing the rice around the shore. Bows ready, the hunters went to collect some ducks and other birds for the feast. A group tended to the fire and drying rack above it, and another person spreading rice on a big canvas to dry in part sun/ part shade. The young girls stirred the buckets full of rice with a flat paddle, trying to be careful not to burn it. Men pounded the rice the girls finished with by lifting a pole and then dropping it along the edge of a barrel. She heard the elder women tossing the rice in the air within the birchbark baskets so the chaff blows away from the seeds. She also knew the younger men were dancing on the rice to separate the edible chaff from the rice. Ishkode did most of the dancing because he could dance the fastest and lightest of everyone. It was time for celebration.

Papakoosigun took a deep breath and stepped from a tree. She flowed to the ancient tree in the middle of the clearing with all eyes following her every move. Her stomach twisting into knots with each step she took.

She had the fairies to thank for the dress. Made by the most skilled fairies, the dress sparkled mischievous of the yellow leaves in the fall with copper flashing throughout as she moved. Designs did not rest on any part of the dress, but it seemed more elegant for it. Her hair was down, but held in place by a simple crown with leaves laced along every inch.

She stopped in front of the group of elders.

"I Papakoosigun will honor my role by doing my best to be strong and cherish our bond as a people. I will respect you all as my friend and ally. I will be generous with my love and laughter. I will be honest with my actions and words. For all to hear I rejoice in taking this role as leader of the people."

She knelt in the grass and offered tobacco to the four directions, to the creator, and to Mother Earth. She gave thanks for her life and her friends. She asked for strength to do what needed to be done.

She knew her world was starting to change drastically and there was nothing she could do to stop it. She was one little kid without her mother earth to stand on. She listened to the wind singing through the trees. "Tell me what I should do because I don't know anymore."

After the ceremony and the feast Papakoosigun went back and tried to sleep. Before she knew it she was dreaming. Someone yanked her out of cold water, but she didn't know who it was. She started hitting whoever grabbed her.

"Papakoosigun! Papakoosigun! Wake up! Ow! Stop it you're hurting me. It's Bagosendam, will you wake up already."

"Bagosendam? I thought you were supposed to be staying with your parents."

"Yeah, well the elders sent them on another mission. I could have stayed in their house, but it seems so empty. Besides the elders thought you could use a guard who knows you and understands you. They have decided to lift the binding spell. If you do not want it to be put back on you had better listen."

"Okay. Should we go to breakfast, I am starving? Are you hungry?"

"Papakoosigun, what were you dreaming about? I am surprised you did not wake up the whole village."

"The dream was nothing and did not make sense."

They walked down to the dining room and found chairs. Ishkode was sitting next to her regular seat. Bagosendam nudged his seat over and put a chair next to hers. Ishkode looked like he might object to this move, but Papakoosigun shook her head slightly.

Nenookaasi stood, "I am happy we are all finally here. I have a few announcements to make. The elders are to return to their clans. They are to see what is happening and fix what needs to be fixed. They will meet back here in six months time. Since I did not get to finish telling all of you about the betrothal I will inform you now. The queen and Aki are betrothed to each other, but the union will not take place until their eighteenth birthdays. Are there any questions?"

Ishkode looked at Papakoosigun, and made to get up to speak, but Bagosendam held him in his chair. She shook her head at Nenookaasi.

"Good, that is all then. We will meet in six months. Safe journey to all."

CHAPTER 10

SHARP DISASTER

When the elders left the room, Ishkode exploded from his chair. It flew back into the wall.

"Thank you, Papakoosigun for the warning. What am I suppose to do now?"

Bagosendam huffed, "It is not her fault. She did not ask for any of this."

"What is she mute as well as blind? She can't answer me herself? This conservation does not concern you, Bagosendam."

Tears slid down Papakoosigun's face. She knew he was going to be mad, but he was furious. "I am sorry, Ishkode. That is all I can say."

She walked out of the room to the stairs and ran up to her room. She heard him stomping up the stairs, but then they stopped. She opened her door a crack to hear what was happening. Ahsin stood on the top step with her hands braced on her hips.

"Listen to me young man. You do not need to go stomping around this house. You need to leave and think about what you said and what you are going to say."

She closed her door slowly and sat against it. She put her head in her hands and screamed in frustration. Then she crawled into bed and wished the day away.

"You need to hurry Papakoosigun, we should not keep the unicorns waiting." Soongede'e leaned down and brushed his sky blue pants straight. He looked fit to met royalty. Papakoosigun did not want to go to the meeting, but he was so excited. She wondered how she can get out of this. Hummm. Maybe.

"What if Bagosendam went instead of me? I could stay here and attend to the business of the village."

"Nice try, Papakoosigun. Bagosendam is going as well, but the unicorns said they wanted to meet you. They will not show up if you are not there. It is only fair, you promised. Maybe we can ask Ishkode if he wants to come."

"Fine, I did promise. Ishkode is busy and does not want to be bothered right now."

"How do you know, you haven't talked to him in weeks? Maybe we can ask Bagosendam to go see."

Bagosendam huffed, "Quit talking about me as if I am not here. Maybe I don't want to go ask. I thank the creator everyday, Papakoosigun that I am an only child."

Soongede'e stuck his tongue out at Bagosendam and wiggled his ears.

Papakoosigun's laugh sent the trees to quivering. "Oh you two are so funny. I don't think you are an only child anymore."

Bagosendam stuck her lower lip out and turned with her arms folded. She felt like pouting now. The traitor.

"Enough you two. I don't want to hear anymore about Ishkode." Papakoosigun looked at Bagosendam with despair in her eyes. Bagosendam leaned forward and rubbed her arm.

She won't have to hear us. You traitor. You could have helped me this once to get them to talk. I would owe you big. I promise.

No way,Soongede'e. I don't want to be see her sad anymore than you do. I let her decision stand, it is not our place. Besides you still owe me for last time when you snuck out of the lodge. Now stop it because she may not hear our thoughts, but she knows what we are doing.

I hear the both of you. I think you need more practice at keeping your thoughts quieter. Please, just drop it.

"I just want to get a drink before we go to the clearing." It was a distraction and stale. Papakoosigun did not want to feel anyone searching her face.

She tried to control her face to not make any face; it was harder than she thought it would be. She squatted in the sand to hide while she composed herself.

Papakoosigun laid her bow and quiver case on the ground beside her. She leaned down, cupped her hands and scooped cool sweet water to her mouth.

Soongede'e sighed, "Why are the unicorns even hiding from the elves now?"

"They are scared and do not know who to trust." Looking at the sky,

Papakoosigun sighed. "It has been thousands of years since the last war with the humans, but the unicorns remember. They believe some of the elves are not satisfied to stay in the villages anymore. We are tainted by the humans."

Bagosendam took a resounding breath. "Are you ready? We must meet with them before sunset."

Soongede'e helped Papakoosigun to her feet.

"Yes, I am ready."

A group of unicorns glided cautiously toward them, but stayed in the shadow of the trees as much as possible. A young unicorn came up to them and bowed to

Papakoosigun and rubbed against Soongede'e.

We are happy to see you, all of you. We are sorry for the caution we have. We know the question you have. We will stay with the centaurs and I think they are planning to move deeper in the forest.

A centaur trotted up beside the unicorns. His deep voice vibrated in Papakoosigun's chest as he addressed their group.

"The unicorn speaks true. We are moving deeper into the mountains and forest. You must beware. The humans will change our world quickly. If it is for the better or it is worse only time will tell."

The unicorns bowed. The young unicorn spoke in their minds with passion.

Thank you all for coming, it was our honor to meet you. We will meet again in the future. Until then be safe.

The centaurs and the unicorns trotted out of the clearing and into the trees, fading from sight. The young unicorn turned once to look back at them before disappearing in the shadows.

The giant Niibin glided with grace into the clearing and rested on the ground next to Papakoosigun and the others.

"I came only for some young giants who are feeling the pressure from the humans moving into the mountains. The humans spread out their homes squeezing us in smaller circles. We need to be careful."

Three young giants walked into the clearing carrying packs as big as a house. Niibin rose up, "I will see you again, but we must be off. I smell humans in the area. Be careful."

The giants left the clearing, their footsteps shook the ground and rumble in the distance. Papakoosigun whipped her head around and stared in shock toward the opposite side of the clearing. Noises of breaking branches announced the humans' arrival. The noise of the giants must have attracted them. She could feel the pain of the trees. How could they be so noisy and destructive? She grabbed Soongede'e hand.

Papakoosigun whispered, "Go hide in the trees. I am right behind you. Hurry young one. No matter what, be quiet."

Soongede'e sprinted into the trees and climbed an old one on the edge of the clearing. Bagosendam climbed up beside him and looked into the clearing. Papakoosigun was moving slowly and limping, because she twisted her ankle. A whooshing noise sounded through the forest and Papakoosigun fell to the ground. Soongede'e was going to jump from the tree, but Bagosendam held her back. She could see Papakoosigun waving them not to with one hand and holding the arrow in her chest with her other hand. They could hear the humans talking.

"What is the matter with you, Matt? You know you are not supposed to fire an arrow until you see what you are firing at clearly. What if you hit a person?"

"I saw movement in the grass up ahead. If it was a deer, I did not want it to get away."

They ran into the clearing and saw Papakoosigun lying on the ground.

"Holy Crap! You did hit a person! This is bad, so bad!"

Matt shouted, "Anyone here? Do you
have your cell? We need to call the
ambulance."

"No, I left my cell in the car. What
are we going to do?"

"We need to see if she is ok. Hurry!"

They started running toward
Papakoosigun when Zhimaagan pumped
her wings with the power of her anger,
circling overhead. She roared her
displeasure and they backed up a few steps.
She landed and crouched over
Papakoosigun and roared again. The
humans had never seen a dragon, but knew
that was what they were staring at. They
turned and ran. Zhimaagan chased them

out of the clearing and Soongede'e skidded on his knees next to Papakoosigun. Papakoosigun wailed in pain when he touched the arrow which was close to her heart. Soongede'e sat back and rocked himself while Bagosendam rubbed his back in comfort.

Zhimaagan came back and dipped her head toward Papkoosigun.

I need to take her back to the village as fast as possible. Bagosendam take Soongede'e and we will meet you there. The humans are gone, so you should be safe, but hurry.

Papakoosigun grabbed Soongede'e's hand. *No he stays with me. I may need him on the flight.*

Fine! Bagosendam get her on my back now!

Papakoosigun passed out on the way to the village. She snapped awake before they started to descend.

"Soongede'e I need you to be strong. Can you do that for me? If the people see you crying it will make them panic."

"Yes, I will do anything as long as you promise to get better."

"I promise to try."

161

By the time they arrived he was composed and calm as he helped her down. The healers had answered Zhimaagan's call and were waiting to help him get her to the ground. They carried her to her room. She saw Soongede'e race toward the forges.

Papakoosigun woke to the sound of voices raised in agitation. One of the healers leaned over her.

"Where are you?"

"Why?"

"I am just curious?"

"We are sitting in my room. Is everything okay? Where is Soongede'e?"

"He is sleeping at the foot of your bed with his sister. Now will you please stop trying to move?"

"Papakoosigun!" Ishkode ran over and pulled the healer away from her.

The healer stared at Ishkode in surprise.

"What is the matter with you, Ishkode? She needs my help."

Ishkode led everyone out of the room. "We need to talk."

Papakoosigun stared at him exhausted and her eyes started to close. Ishkode grabbed her hand.

"Papakoosigun, I have something to tell you. Listen to the trees and then listen to me."

"The trees are telling me change is coming fast."

"Yes, change is coming and I need you to stay with me from now on. You always find trouble when we are apart."

"I seem to find trouble even when I am with you."

"I am sorry for getting so mad; I know it was not your fault. What would I do if you were with Aki? I want to stay and take care of you."

"I don't believe you. I am alone. What am I going to do?"

"You are never alone. I am here. Soongede'e is here. Bagosendam is here. We will take care of you."

"You promise?"

"I promise."

Zhimaagan poked her head in the window.

You are forgetting me. I think if you keep this up Papakoosigun. The elders are never going to let you even leave this house.

Papakoosigun grinned and grabbed nut muffins off a tray beside her, "They could try, right? You were seen by humans. What are we going to do about that?"

Papakoosigun turned her head toward Zhimaagan and felt the happiness coming from her. Zhimaagan gave a smile, which to anyone else would have seemed more like a snarl.

I have been worried about you not them. The humans do not remember ever seeing a dragon. It was a storm in the forest and they were lost. How goes it, little one?

Papakoosigun sighed, wanting to go over to Zhimaagan and laid her head against her friend's hide. *I am stiff and I hurt, but I am alive. I am worried, tired and feel that I could be doing more. But other than, I am doing fine.*

Zhimaagan sat quiet and still for a long time, almost to the point where Papakoosigun thought she fell asleep. Zhiimaagan finally shifted.

He will be okay, Papakoosigun. Do not worry so much. I will watch over him and his little sister. Ishkode has something for you.

He was holding out a necklace sparkling in the late sun light.

"I made this for you. It took me awhile to find all of the pieces I wanted. It is for our friendship and to protect you. Zhimaagan and I put some magic inside the biggest stone, so as long as you wear it you will be safe."

"Wow! Thank you so much. I know it must have taken you a long time to make. It looks to be made with care and I will wear it with care. It is beautiful and look it matches my hair."

Ishkode grinned in delight.

"It is almost time for the berry gathering, Papakoosigun. I know how much you use to love to gather as many as you could of every type. Will we join in this year? You should be better by then."

"We will have to see, Ishkode. Right now I think it is time for a snack and a rest."

CHAPTER 11

HUNTED

Waawaabashkiki started coming into the area of the village. At first it was one or two sightings, which was normal. Then more sightings were being reported, for the time of year and the location of the sightings it was worrisome. The sightings were getting closer and closer to the village and they surrounded the village. It was suspected they were looking for a certain girl; they grabbed only girls with red hair.

They searched the inside of their upper arms looking for her birthmark as proof.

There were few people who knew of her birthmark. They were all under suspicion. Everyone in the village was watchful and scared.

As they began to bed down they heard a terrible noise. It was like all the trees in the forest were being torn from the ground or knock away as if they were merely twigs. Papakoosigun ran out of the house at the sound and met Ishkode at the door.

He was whispering and gesturing, "You need to take the young ones and hide.

Don't hide in the crown home, which is the first place they will look."

"How do you know they are looking for me?"

"I don't know for certain, it is just a feeling. I will feel better if you are hiding. Now go. They are getting closer."

Papakoosigun crept to the tree branches of the crown home. She led Soongede'e carrying his sister in her cradleboard and Bagosendam through the trees. They moved quickly and quietly.

There was sound below them so they kept going. Finally they were well away from the village, close to the river. They rested on a large branch high off the ground. Soongede'e tied all of them to the tree.

"Papakoosigun, you should rest. I will keep watch."

There was a crashing roar through the forest and then they saw a blur come at them in the tree tops.

Ishkode skidded to a halt, whipped out his knife and sliced the ropes. "I followed the Waawaabashkiki. They are after you and they are coming now. We must go to the river."

CHAPTER 12

ESCAPE

The sound came closer. They had not been fast enough, and they knew that they were spotted.

Papakoosigun dragged the young ones to the river's edge. They all gave each other frighten looks. Ishkode turned to Soongede'e.

"I will take Wigwaasi; you jump in the river and swim for the opposite bank as soon as you can. Meet us at the spring of dragon tears. Ija, jump now."

Soongede'e dove in the water with a cry. Ishkode tied Bagosendam to Papakoosigun.

"Take care of each other."

He then scooped up Wigwaasi in the cradleboard. As he jumped in the water he jerked Bagosendam and Papakoosigun in. As they fell into the icy dark waters Papakoosigun gave a mighty cry. At the same moment that they were jerked toward the water Bagosendam looked back. As they surfaced and were carried away, Bagosendam looked back to their camp and

175

saw in the firelight a sight that made her cringe and grab tighter to Papakoosigun.

Standing on the shore and swarming their tree like giant insects were what she knew to be the Waabashkiki. Bikwak was fighting them as she passed a bend, she saw him go down. She had only heard of these creatures in stories, but the way they were described there could be no question.

These creatures came from the swamp lands past the plains and were eight to ten feet tall with bulging muscles in their necks, arms and legs. Each had a large horn that came out of the middle of the head and tiny spikes behind it going from the horn down their backs. Their hands were big enough for her to curl up comfortably in, and that thought sent shivers up her spine. They had large orb like eyes and razor sharp teeth.

All those eyes were now following her and her family downstream. They would not follow; water was the one thing that they feared because it was deep. They were large and heavy and could not swim, so for now her family was safe.

CHAPTER 13

ABANDONED

The currents were strong and while they were swimming with the current and singing to the water the binding broke that held Bagosendam to Papakoosigun.

Papakoosigun could not keep herself above water and search for Bagosendam to grab at the same time.

With a cry of frustration,
"Bagosendam! Bagosendam!"

She slapped the water searching the area around her with her hands. She gasped as her hand found Bagosendam's dress. Papakoosigun held on with a death grip with fear pouring over along with the water. The water was getting rougher and turning into rapids. Bagosendam tried repeated times to get to the water's edge, but was bogged down and could not see where to go.

Bagosendam wailed in frustration and exhaustion and kept grabbing Papakoosigun's hand to make sure she had a good grip.

"Just hang on, Bagosendam. Do you hear me? Just hang on."

"I'm trying. Papakoosigun we are close to the bank. I see a log hanging over the water. When I say, hold tight. I am going to reach up. Now."

Bagosendam reached up and seized the log. The force of Bagosendam stopping wrenched her dress from Papakoosigun's cold hands. Papakoosigun's scream echoed in the night. She tried to get back to Bagosendam, but the current was too strong.

"Papakoosigun!"

"Bagosendam, help me!"

As Papakoosigun was carried away in the dark screaming, she went under. Her screams were cut short. She was panicking and couldn't think. When she went under,her head hit a rock hidden below the surface.

She woke with a start screaming for her family.

CHAPTER 14

ENEMY TERRITORY

The woman standing over her covered her mouth, "You need to be quiet, or your scream will make the others hungry."

The scream was cut short, "Who are you? What are you going to do with me?"

"I know elvish, but you no speak it, you speak Waabashkiki words, or no talk. Understand?"

"Yes."

"Good, come with me. What they call you?"

"I don't remember."

"We call you, Mnisose because that is where I found you." The woman grinned; her sharp teeth making her look fierce. "Smart, am I not?"

She followed the woman like a stray puppy to a hut that was made of mud and grasses from the surrounding area. It was a huge hut; she could enter without ducking her six foot frame even a little.

"Wait here, Mnisose. I will be back soon." The woman said this slow and loud as she was hard of hearing.

She knew Mnisose wasn't even close to her name, but no matter how hard she tried she could not remember her real name. She wondered if her sight was always gone or if the accident that had dropped her here was the case. At least she could make out shapes and shadows, which for some reason she thought was a vast improvement.

The woman stomped back to her; at least she hoped it was the woman. It sounded the same, but just in case she moved closer to the wall.

"What you doing? I told you to stay here, not over there! You need to listen."

"I am sorry I did not know who was coming, I can't see except shapes and shadows. I was scared."

"No need to be scared, you belong to me and I am great warrior woman in our tribe."

"What are you called?"

"I am called Ocinsica Ceya. You need to come here and clean up."

Ocinsica Ceya grabbed her hand and led her over toward the middle of the hut. She put Mnisose's hand in warm water, making the water splash. She was moving her hand to show her how big the tub was and how deep. She could lay or sit in it comfortably.

"Thank you, Ocinsica Ceya. I will bathe."

She lay in the water and let the warm water soak into her, easing the aches that she had not realized she had. She washed her hair with yucca root, and found bruises

on her arms, legs, stomach and she was
pretty sure on her back. She felt her head as
she washed her hair. There was a big knot
right behind her ear. It was very tender to
the touch. She stood in the tub and swayed,
as she felt waves of nausea hit her. She
thought she might get sick. Then she felt a
big hand steady her and hand her a rough
piece of cloth.

She dried and dressed quickly. The
clothes given to her were not her own, but
must have been a child's because they fit if a
little baggie. She tied a belt around her
waist. Ocinsica Ceya dragged her toward the
door and made her sit right outside the

door. Then a shorter shadow came at her and she flinched onto Ocinsica Ceya.

"It's okay you silly little creature. This is our elder, a healing woman who can help you. Sit still."

Mnisose was still scared, but she sat up straight, watching the shadow grow closer and closer. The shadow was smaller than Ocinsica Ceya's shadow and spoke in a whispery voice.

"Poor thing, so little. It is a surprise that she made it down the river with only bumps and bruises. Look at me young one. Look at grandmother, look at Unci. Good girl."

"Her eyes are cloudy, but I see a hint of green trying to escape. I may be able to help her eyes, but let's look at her head first."

The old woman touched her head gently. Then she searched her arms and legs. Then she turned away and Mnisose could hear her rummaging in a bag.

"This is for the head; this is for the bruises and this. This is for your eyes, you are lucky. I don't always have this medicine."

Unci pushed a cup that radiated heat and smelled minty with a slight honey smell into her face. She quickly grabbed the cup

189

before it was spilled and noticed a relief to her pounding head. Then Unci rubbed some smelly sticky paste into her bruises that made her think of the earth and the smell of a crushed leaf. Mnisose was happy when the aches slowly receded.

"Drink it all up, please. Good girl. Now, we must lay you down. I must put this in your eyes and then we are going to wrap them tight so no light gets in. Then you sleep."

Mnisose drank the cup offered to her without questions. She was led into the hut and laid down. They put liquid into her eyes and then wrapped them tight, making her eyes water with the little sting that went with the drops. By the time they were done she was drifting to sleep.

"Thank you." She whispered and then surrendered to the blackness.

CHAPTER 15

RIVER

She was made to stay in the hut for weeks and only led out for a walk once a day. She knew a child led her on these walks because her hand fit into hers snuggly. Mnisose was getting tired of the hut; she knew the entire room by touch. She felt trapped and tried to plead her case to Ocinsica Ceya again.

"Please, Ocinsica Ceya if you let me out more I promise not to go far. I don't want to stay in here anymore."

"Stop asking. You tire me. You sound like a baby, always asking questions. Unci will say when you leave."

The old woman walked in the hut as if she was called. She led Mnisose to her mat and made her sit down.

"We will see today, stop bothering Ocinsica Ceya. She is worrying about the village right now. The humans have not found us, but without a lot of magic, they may one day. Ocinsica Ceya is worried it is soon. Sit still."

Unci unwrapped her eyes and she blinked at the brightness that assaulted her eyes, making them water.

She looked around her, "Wow, I can see. I cannot believe you fixed my eyes! Everything is so bright! It hurts a little though."

Unci patted her arm, "Calm, little one. Too loud. But you are welcome and the pain will go away when you get use to it."

She looked into Unci's face and smiled. She could see everything in fine detail.

"Now you can help the camp and learn, young one. Here, let me braid your hair."

Mnisose was excited to leave the hut and explore the village and surrounding area. It was almost time for her walk and she could not wait. She turned and saw a young female Waabashkiki walking toward her. She was followed by a group of ten or twelve others. She bowed her head at Mnisose before stopping, and then she held out her hand. The others had staffs in their hands and she studied them warily. They bowed their heads, but made no move toward her.

They started to make their rounds around the village and she stared with wide-eyed wonder at everything. It was a big settlement. She watched people making weapons, cooking, making household items. Some of the people glared at her and then they met her eyes and looked away in a huff with a slight trace of fear emitting off of them.

They rounded a corner and she was pulled to a stop. The others of the group stepped in front of her and took a defensive stance. There were other young ones of various ages blocking the path. Some looked close to adulthood. The ones who were defending her looked about half the size. She began to worry.

The bullies started throwing rocks, aiming at her and the female who had her hand. The rocks never found their targets. Her protectors were whirling their staffs and knocking the rocks away.

One rock came past the others and was heading right for her guide when Mnisose raised her hand. The rock slowed down and then came to rest in her hand.

"Enough!"

All of them saw what happened and the bullies scattered faster than leaves in autumn.

"Please, tell me. What was that about? Do I get to know the names of my protectors? Have you done this every day since I have been here? Why have none of you spoken?"

"You are not welcomed here; you are not one of us. My name is Can Can, the others don't want you to know their names yet, so you can call them numbers. You know 1, 2, 3, and 4. We have been the ones to walk you and we spoke because there was nothing to say."

Her guides lead her quickly back toward the hut. Can Can shuddered when Ocinsica Ceya came into view.

"It happened again, Ocinsica Ceya. We need to take her for walks away from the village. No one wants her here, and when the men return it could mean trouble."

"Fine, do what needs to be done. I will deal with the men when the time comes."

CHAPTER 16

NIIMII

So my guides started taking me out of the village for walks. They lived in beautiful country, andshe was surprised that she did not see other people or creatures around. She heard this pitiful little timid screech. She searched the trees around her, but all she saw were leaves. Suddenly, a small ball of fluff flew at her.

My name is Niimii. Help me. I am all alone. Some human hunters killed my mother with an arrow.

She remembered hearing something close to this. Someone, some person she used to know was killed by human hunters. She tried to grab the memory, but it faded until all she could do was cuddle the small fluff.

"Ssshh. It's okay. I have you. What am I going to do with you?"

I don't know. Fly with me?

"I don't know how to fly little one, but I bet it is cool. You can share it with me when you are older."

Niimi was humming along with her before she even realized she was humming.

"Are you hungry, Niimii?"

Yes, it has been many days since I lost my mother.

She started looking around in the trees and the ground. She saw some fruit in the tree and sang to it that she was hungry and can she please have some of its fruit. Two pieces of fruit dropped into her hands.

She lifted a log and found some grubs for Niimii. He shook his beak in disgust, but he was hungry.

I am a kestrel and we eat mice and snakes. We do not eat grubs and they smell yucky.

"I am sorry, but grubs are all I can hunt right now. We have to get back to the village, and I need to think of what to tell Ocinsica Ceya."

He snuggled into her arms and went to sleep as they walked back. She had someone who needed her.

I am here to protect you.

"Okay, little one. You are my official protector. Now sleep."

She made him a nest next to her bed and fed him all she could, and he grew over the weeks that she cared for him. He no longer nestled in her arms except for right before she went to bed. He sat on her shoulder and studied all the creatures that came near his girl.

I do not like all of these Waabashkiki. Some of them are not good at all.

"I am fine; none of them have hurt me. Relax, Niimii."

No.

"Fine, be that way." She grinned as he ruffled his feathers in a huff.

CHAPTER 17

DIZZY DISPLAY

She went for a walk in the woods, alone for once. Her guides had other chores that needed to be done. She was happy to find a little peace and quiet away from everyone except Niimii. She took a pack with her and decided to harvest food for her friends back in the village.

She found some nuts and berries and gathered them until her bag was almost full.

Then she decided to explore a little further than she normally would have with her guides. Her guides always making her turn back at a certain point saying there was nothing interesting further.

She continued walking until she heard this rushing sound and found a waterfall. She thought this was very interesting, and decided she was going to tell the others when she got back. She heard a whispering laughter and wondered where it came from. Nothing seems to be around her except the birds flirting around from branch to branch. She looked around herself and laughed because even though

she still did not remember anything, she
knew she was home.

Somehow that was the first thought
that popped in her head. Niimii grew
restless on her shoulder.

*Someone or something is watching
our every move. They are waiting for
something.*

"What?"

I don't know.

The sun had faded behind some
clouds low in the western sky; she looked
up not realizing how late it was. She needed

to get back to the camp before true darkness set in; the swamp was not friendly at night.

When she looked in the direction of the camp there was a wall of lights blocking her way. The lights seemed to be dancing and every so often they danced close together. She moved closer and knew where the whispering laughter came from. She could hear music coming from somewhere near. As she got closer to the lights she realized it wasn't just lights and that the lights were only a few of what they were. There were a lot of them that did not have lights at all.

They were fairies; the lights were sealed lanterns that let off a glow. Some of the fairies were holding them as they danced by themselves and with each other.

They were beautiful, the males and the females. Little sculptured people with delicate wings. They floated on the wind, the wind seemed to be dancing with them and carrying them around the meadow. The music was their voices that carried on the wind.

"Niimii, I am sure they are the whispering that we heard."

Yes.

He tensed on her shoulder and clenched tight. The fairies gathered around her in a tight circle, and all begin talking at once.

"You are our friend."

"I am so happy to meet you."

"Please, come dance with us."

She held up her hands and then sighed.

"It sounds like fun, but I need to get back to the Waabashkiki camp. I am already running late."

The fairies swirled faster and faster in distress.

"No, you cannot go. You are an elf, a fairy friend. You do not belong in that village. You have to stay with us."

"I have to get back. Sorry."

The fairies would not let her past. She was starting to get dizzy and went down on her knees and placed her hands on the ground.

"Fairies! You need to stop, I am getting dizzy. I . . ."

The fairies did not stop and they put both the girl and the bird to sleep. They could not move her. Some of them guarded and some of them went quickly for the elves for help. They had to stop her from returning to the Waabashkiki village, no matter what.

CHAPTER 18

TAKEN

The fairies were guarding the girl waiting for the other fairies to return with the elves, when they heard noises. Loud noises and a stench that made their wings wilt. Ogres!

What where they going to do with the girl? Then they heard a sound coming from the opposite direction. The elves! The fairies stared in the direction of the new noise, wishing they would hurry. Waabashkiki came out of the woods and the fairies went into a frenzy. This was bad.

The Waabashkiki spotted the girl on the ground and hurried over to her. One of them lifted her up into her arms, and then went flying as an ogre came out of the woods swinging his club. The girl fell to the ground with a thud.

The ogre roared, "Mine! My pretty."

The Waabashkiki grouped in front of the girl and crouched into fighting stance.

"She is not yours. Go away!"

"MINE!"

The ogre did not want to talk anymore and swung his club at the Ocinsica Ceya; she jumped back and swung her sword, cutting the ogre.

Another ogre came out of the woods with a huge, crude sword. He spun around body and sword and sliced Ocinsica Ceya's head away from her body. The old warrior woman died instantly.

The Waabashkiki howled in disbelief and the ogres took advantage of their shock. The ogres grabbed the girl and ran away into the woods. The Waabashkiki did not even give chase; they sat on the ground around Ocinsica Ceya.

The ogres took the girl to their cave, and wondered why she still slept. It was no fun if they did not scream. They did not know what to do with her so they dumped her in the back of the cave and forgot all about her.

She woke slowly from her sleep feeling sore and hungry. She heard gruff, rough voices talking in whispers.

"Mikwam say come back. Say we strong."

"Mikwam not come back, long time. She not care anymore."

"We need to fight and she will come back. You see."

"Ok. Who we fight?"

"Elves, humans, who care."

"I tired, go sleep now."

She did not hear anything and then loud snores filled the cave. The snores made her eardrums hum and hurt. She slowly crept out of where they put her only to find, not all of the ogres went to sleep.

"Pretty hair, come."

"No thanks, I think I will go now."

"No stay here."

He grabbed her arm and made her sit by him. She huffed and thought about how she could get free.

He fell asleep with her hair twisted and clenched tightly in his hand. She knew she was not going anywhere. She would have cut her hair to get free, but nothing sharp was within reach. She tried to pull away, but he would yank her closer each time. She lay still and wondered what she was going to do. How was she going to get free? How was she going to get away from this camp that was surrounded by hundreds of ogres?

A young ogre crept closer to the girl keeping to the shadows. Her hair was pretty, like a fire and he loved staring at fires. He had been staring at her all night. He waited all night until the others were asleep.

He slowly unwound her hair from the leader's hand. He led her away from the fire and handed her a cape. He put his head close to hers and started whispering. He did not smell like the other ogres, he smelled like earth and rain.

"You go before light comes. I like you, no like Mud. This cape magic, like stone. Hide you, no one find you."

She braided a small piece of her hair and then reached over and grabbed the knife from his belt. She cut the braid off and gave it to him and smiled, "Thank you."

She crept off slowly into the hills trying not to touch any of the ogres. She crept up the hill and then stopped. She curled up and covered with the cape, she hoped it worked. When the sun came up, the ogres woke in an uproar. They stomped around looking and then took off down the hill toward the river. They found a red hair going in that direction. That little ogre was still helping her. There was goodness in every race she met.

She would wait to make sure all of the ogres were gone before she moved again. She wanted to head back to the camp as soon as she could. She planned to stay as far away from that fairy meadow as she could.

CHAPTER 19

UNSHAKABLE LOSS

Mnisose knew the direction of the
Waabashkiki camp and she started toward
it as soon as the area was clear. She
followed the river and climbed a tree
anytime she heard or smelled an ogre
coming toward her. It was slow and took
her a long time. When she came near the
fairy meadow she went around and ran into
a group of elves.

"There you are, we have been looking everywhere for you." A young man sighed with relief. "We can go back to the village now."

"I can't go with you anywhere; I have to get back to my camp and people."

He looked confused, "What camp do you mean?"

"I mean the Wabashkiki camp near the swamps. I need to see Ocinsica Ceya, she will be worried."

"You don't belong there with those creatures, you belong with us. Your own kind."

"I can see what you mean to a point, but I still need to get back. You don't seem to understand, she will be worried."

"Ocinsica Ceya was killed by an ogre."

"How do you know? I don't believe you. I want to see for myself. You just don't want me to go back there. You lie!"

"I am elf and I did not lie. You lie to yourself now. Fine, we will go to the meadow and show you."

He stomped as he lead the way to the meadow, mumbling under his breath. He gestured to the far side of the meadow with his hand and I saw a shape shrouded with cloth and a group of Wabashkiki surrounding it. She walked slowly toward the group, when Can Can turned around.

She jumped up and ran at them, "What are you doing here? You don't belong here! We are mourning Ocinsica Ceya." She turned a glare and snarled at Mnisose, "This is your fault. She would still be here if the ogres didn't want you. Go away!"

Mnisose's face dropped and tears streamed down her cheeks, "I'm so sorry."

The snarl never left Can Can's face, "Those are just words; they don't change the past. Just go away. Now!"

"I will leave."

Mnisose turned and slumped down as she stumbled away. As she neared the edge of the clearing, a flutter caught her attention. Niimii flew to her shoulder and landed with a thump. He steadied himself and then rubbed his head against her cheeks.

Don't cry, I am here.

"It was my fault Niimii, how can I not be sad. I am glad you are okay, I was so worried."

She kept walking in the opposite direction from the Wabashkiki when she felt a hand on her shoulder. She spun around and grabbed the hand and shoved the owner away. Niimii screamed in indignation and then again in protection at the man who touched Mnisose. He spread his wings and they brushed her head as he tried to look fierce.

All of the elves took a step back, but then he caught himself and stood up straight, "We need to go this way."

She glared, "Fine go that way, I want to go this way."

"If you don't come with us by your choice, then we will have to make you.

There are more of us. Please, we don't want to have to do that."

"I do not want to go! Don't you understand! Are you listening?"

"We understand what you want, but it is not going to matter."

Some of elves started to surround her, She searched around her and saw there were too many of them.

"Okay, I will go. Lead the way."

CHAPTER 20

FORGOTTEN HOME

Mnisose followed them until they walked up to a large lake surrounded by trees. Then they started following the water's edge. She trailed the others at a slower pace so that she could take in all the sights she was passing.

All of the homes were using the trees without harming them. She walked up to a large tree growing from the middle of a clearing. A man and a woman were waiting to meet the group. They nodded to the others who shifted to the side and then bowed deeply to Mnisose. They smiled at her.

"Welcome home, my lady."

"Where am I?"

"You are in the village of the forest elves."

"Why am I here? You called me, my lady; do you know who I am?"

"You are here because you are a lost forest elf. You are a lady and that is why I call you my lady. I know who you are, but

we must take this slow. I know your name,
it is Papakoosigun."

She rolled the name on her tongue,
"Papakoosigun."

She got a flash of someone shouting
that name in playfulness, but nothing else.

"Awegwen nin, I don't know who I
am. It sounds familiar, but I just don't
know."

"It may take time for you to heal,
please come and rest."

They lead her to the huge tree and
then inside to a room. She could not rest
and felt a pull to move in a certain

direction. She started pacing the room and then decided to go explore the area. She knew her steps were being noticed and watched, and she was being followed.

She walked into the forest for a time and then came upon a big river. She looked at the water and wondered why this area seemed to call her. She looked back and saw the eyes of her pursuers in the moonlight. She felt at home in the trees, but she knew that those people would not let her be in peace.

She had the urge to touch the rocks at her feet, so she bent down and ran her hands over them. She picked up one rock and then sighed as she placed it in her pouch. More flashes came to her of a town on the coast and people faces. Maybe this stone was the key to unlocking her memory.

She wondered if she could cross the river or leave the forest. She wanted to find a forest with inhabitants that would not bother her. She started walking along the river. When the sun was lighting the sky she found what she was looking for.

The edge of the forest ended in a bend of the river. She looked past the river and saw plains as far as the eye could see. The plains looked vast with interruptions every so often with hills or trees.

She went to place her foot in the water and was hit by a blast of air and light. It was not that strong, but it was enough to knock her off her feet. Her pursuers came close; the young elves were charged with watching over her.

They did not want to hurt her, but they felt that what happened to her was a small price to pay for her safety. They knew she was scared not only of them, but of the past she did not remember. The tallest one lifted her in his arms and carried her back to the great tree.

He carried her as if she was a delicate flower for the elders would not be happy if anything was to happen to this fragile woman. She was the picture of natural beauty with large emerald green eyes and her fine artful features of the face. He took notice of her fire bright hair framing her face and swinging against his arm. He felt her song that flowed through her veins and knew she was important, somehow.

They stepped back toward the center of their clearing in a quarter of the time than the going. The people of the clan came closer and the elders let out a gasp. One of the elders grabbed her hands and studied her fingertips. The blue that hidden by the dirt of travel mean she could only be one person. She must be the new queen and was more important than any of them first thought.

The one who carried her laid her gently on the bed in a room within the large tree. As he was attending to this, a woman set out some clothes on the stool for her. The queen had been through a lot and was fragile and seemed like a little doll that a girl would carry around by the arm.

When the young man departed the woman started to sponge off the travel dirt. The woman laid a wet washcloth on her forehead. Then she left to get some food for when Papakoosigun woke up. The woman sat in the chair beside the bed and waited for the queen to wake.

Papakoosigun was awake, but she was scared to open her eyes. So she moved her hands around her and her surroundings, she was in a soft bed. She had only been dreaming of all the horrible things that happened. She sensed someone near her and without realizing it she cried out, "Ocinsica Ceya."

She popped open her eyes and got a shock. She was in a beautiful room and a beautiful dress was sitting on a stool. The biggest shock was the woman who sat watching her. She had coppery blond hair and skin as fair as the first snow of winter season. She had a striking beauty. The way the woman had set her hair helped to boast her pointed ears.

The woman smiled at her and said, "Aniibiish Ndishnikaaz, my name is Aniibiish, Leaf." She smiled again and sat there for a minute. "Since you are awake would you like to wash and dress? Then you can eat the food I brought for you, my lady."

She held out her hand and Papakoosigun took it. Aniibiish lead her behind a screen where a hot tub waited for her. She sat in the tub until the water grew cold, washed quickly and then dressed in the dress Aniibiish handed her. The dress seemed to be woven from a delicate spider's web and shone with the light of the moonlight.

As they walked out of the door to the room, her escorts were waiting outside and followed behind them as they continued walking. Aniibiish led her to a gathering table with a group of elders. She was glad she ate in her room because now her stomach was churning in nervousness.

The female began, "Now that you are rested, we can get to know one another. My name is Nenookaasi. We know each other.

We sent for a friend of yours, hoping this will help you gain your memory back."

One of the older males grinned, "You are probably anxious to meet this person, but they will not be here for a couple days. So . . . you can explore the village and become comfortable here. You escorts will show you around."

Nenookaasi pointed to the two who had waited outside of her room and followed them down. "The tall one is Bikwak and the shorter one is Aki. They will stay with you everywhere you go except your room. So if you have any questions, I am sure they can answer them."

"Thank you, but I don't think I need anyone to show me around."

"Humor us and let them guide you or we will have to insist you stay in your room."

"Fine."

Papakoosigun walked out of the building before the other two realized and they raced to catch up to her. She knew they meant well, but this was ridiculous. She did not speak to them and then went back to her room tired of her shadows. She stayed in her room for days, taking her food on the one small table in there. She did not want to leave if they were going to guard her. She knew they acted like friends, but she felt like a prisoner.

A knock came to the door; she thought it was maybe Aniibiish. Aniibiish said that if Papakoosigun insisted on staying in the room they might as well have something to read, so she went to the library. She went to the door and opened it, but it was not Aniibiish standing in front of her.

EPILOGUE
A START

Ishkode was at the door, Papakoosigun did not know where the name came from, but it was there suddenly in her mind.

"Ishkode?"

He fell to his knees in front of her, "Oh, thank the creator. I thought you were gone."

He stood up and grabbed her in a hug, "They told me you lost your memory.

Don't worry I will help you get it back . . . somehow."

Aki was fuming, "You should not grab the queen like that. It is not right."

Ishkode glared at him, "She is my friend and I was worried, not that I need to explain anything I do to you."

Papakoosigun held Ishkode's hand and led him into her rooms, firmly closing the door on Aki's face. She turned to Ishkode and grinned.

"I wanted to do that since I got here. They won't let me leave unless they are with me. I don't know who I am. Then these people tell don't do this or that. Ugg. It is frustrating."

"Do you remember me? You said my name."

"I remembered that and I know you are a friend, but other than that I can't remember anything."

"What have you been up to?"

"I lived with the Wabashkiki, then the fairies put me to sleep, I woke up in an ogre camp, escaped, was taken by these elves and have not left this room. What about you?"

"Wait, I want to hear more."

Papakoosigun and Ishkode spent most of the day and night talking about what happened to her. Then her questions started to flow.

"Where do I live? Where is my family? How do we know each other? How long have we known each other?"

"You live in California, and I think some of your family is on the Forgotten Island. We met when you came to live in my town. We have known each other for about a year now."

"Why can't I remember?"

"You will. But for now remember this. Akina inawem, akina manidoog, akina gikendaagozi, akina mikwendaagozi."

He started to tell her everything he knew. She had him, she had her token, and she had a start at remembering. Where will she go from here?

NAMES

Papakoosigun – (Papa-coo-see-goon) –
Willow (forest elf)

Biboon – (Bee-boon) – Winter (giant,
teacher of Papakoosigun)- decreased

Opichi – (O-pee-chee) – Robin (forest elf,
twin brother to Papakoosigun)

Jean – (Anishinaabe Native American,
friend of Papakoosigun)

Ishkode – (Ish-coal-day) – Fire (fire elf,
friend of Papakoosigun)

Mikwam – (Mic-wam) – Ice (banished ice
elf, enemy of Papakoosigun)- made human

Bikwak – (Bee-kwaak) – Arrow (forest elf,
guard of Papakoosigun)

Mitigwaab – (Me-tig-waab) – Bow (guard
of Papakoosigun)

Bagosendam – (Bay-go-seen-daam) – Hope (elemental elf, friend of Papakoosigun)

Niibin – (knee-bin) – Summer (giant, son of Biboon, friend of Papakoosigun)

Nenookaasi – (knee-noo-kaa-see) – Hummingbird (speakers of the ambassadors/elders of the elves)

Aki – (Ah-key) – Earth (cave elf ambassador/elder, betrothed to Papakoosigun)

Ziibi – (Zee-bee) – River (water elf ambassador/elder, friend to Papakoosigun)

Dakaagamin – (Bay-kaa-gay-min) – Cold (ice elf ambassador)

Waawaatesi – Firefly (Waa-waa-key-see) – (fire elf ambassador/elder)

Bingwi – Sand (Bin-gwi) – (desert elf ambassador/elder)

Aanakwad – Cloud (Ah-nah-kwad) – (mountain elf ambassador/elder)

Aniibiish – Leaf (Ah-knee-biish) – (caretaker of Papakoosigun)

Zhimaagan – (Zee-maa-gan) – Spear (dragon, protector of the forest elf clan)

Ahsin – (Ah-sin) – Stone (dwarf, caretaker of Papakoosigun on island)

Rosha – (Row-sha) – (master dwarf, teacher of Papakoosigun)

Waabashkiki – (Waa-baash-key-key) – beings that live in the swamp

Mniosose – (Mni-o-so-see) – River (Name of Papakoosigun in Waabashkiki)

Ocinsica Ceya – (O-cin-si-ca Chee- ya) – Fierce Cry (female Waabashkiki warrior)

Can Can – (can – can) Shaker (young female Waabaskkiki)

Unci – (Un-chi)- Grandmother (old female Waabashkiki elder)

PHRASES and WORDS

Ani – Hi

Awibaa - be calm

Eya – Yes

Daga – Please

Noongoom – Now

Baamaapi – Until later

Meegwetch – Thank you

Giishkowe – Stop crying

Biineshiinh- bird

Asabikeshiinh– spider

Akina inawem, akina manidoog, akina
gikendaagozi, akina mikwendaagozi – All

related, all spirits, all known, all
remembered.

ACKNOWLEDGMENTS

This is my second book now and I have to say that these books would not be possible without some very special people.

I want to give a big Miigwetch to all those who have supported me through this experience. Thank you for all the love, support, understanding and tolerance.

I would like to give a special thank you to Gerard, my husband and best friend for your honesty, advice and help with all aspects of this book. You have supported me in every new adventure I wanted to try and I appreciate it. I love you.

I want to thank my three children, J. Janis, E. Janis, and W. Janis, for listening to the stories over and over again. Thank you for giving your questions and opinions freely. Also thank you for sharing your laughs and love.

Thank you to my sister, Heather for reading my book and giving me advice, which I took to heart. Thank you for being so supportive. Thank you for taking the time out of your busy schedule to help me with this dream. I love you and could not have asked for a better sister.

Thank you to my friend and I would say mentor, JC Phelps. Who took time away from her book writing to give me advice. She still takes the time to hear me voice my concerns. I want to thank her from the bottom of my heart.

I would also like to thank my friends and editors, Megan Holtz and Jan Keaton. You have encouraged and supported. You taken the time to read my book and point out the mistakes with glee to my book that I would not have gotten anywhere else. Thank you.

And finally, I want to acknowledge all the fans who have read this book. I hope it brings you into the Elvin world. Meegwetch for reading.

ABOUT THE AUTHOR

V. R. Janis was raised on the Pine Ridge Indian Reservation most of her life. She is part of the Ojibwe tribe from Northern Michigan.

This is her second book of the Hidden Magic Trilogy. The first book is **Hidden Power**. She has also published a book of poetry and photography called **Native Me**.

The goal was to bring the meaning of the culture with the imagination of fantasy to life.

Her husband and children have inspired her. She is proud to teach her children nothing is impossible.

http://vrjanis.wix.com/author-photographer

https://www.facebook.com/authorVRJanis

www.etsy.com/shop/OjibweWonders

email: vrjanis@yahoo.com